JACK
King of the Dogs

SHEILA MOLLOY

WITH ILLUSTRATIONS BY
MICHAEL MOLLOY

PUBLISHED BY
CAN OF WORMS KIDS PRESS
LONDON

JACK: King of the Dogs
1st Edition
Published by Can of Worms Kids Press 2004

Can of Worms Enterprises Ltd
1 Sutherland Walk
London SE17 3EF, UK

Tel: (0044) 845 1233971
Email: info@canofwormspress.co.uk
Website: www.canofwormspress.co.uk

ISBN: 1 904872-30-1
Copyright © 2004 Sheila Molloy
Illustrations Copyright © 2004 Michael Molloy

British Library Cataloguing in Publication Data
A catalogue record for this book is available from the British Library.

Printed and bound in Great Britain

Cover and text design by Alison Eddy on behalf
of Can of Worms Design Group

To my mum

Joan Neal

ACKNOWLEDGEMENTS

THE AUTHOR

SHEILA MOLLOY is a freelance writer and former production editor
and writer for the Daily Express Woman section. She has been a Fleet Street
journalist for 30 years.

One of her articles for the Daily Mail Saturday magazine asking readers
for support to bring home a stray dog from Lefkos raised £10,000 which
was used to help the Greek island's strays.

Sheila lives in South London with her husband Geoff Compton and has
two grown-up children: Michael – who illustrated her book – and Annelise.

After her black labrador Jack died five years ago a bench was erected
on Hampstead Heath in his memory. It is the magic bench in this book.

THE ILLUSTRATOR

Illustrator and musician MICHAEL MOLLOY lives in Crouch End, North
London – he's the James in the book and Sheila's son.

The Author would like to thank Geoff, Michael, Annelise and Carrie for
all their love and support, Toby for his blind faith and Dave Wilson of
The Times for making Jack's bench a reality.

JACK
King the of Dogs

■ CHAPTER ONE ■

THE CHOICE

James shot upright in bed, his heart thumping and his fists clenching the duvet. The nightmare had woken him up yet again and it always played out the same way.

He'd be asleep but when he opened his eyes the room would be covered in a thick, white fog. His mouth would open to scream for help but the fog would rush in, choking him and stinging his eyes. Then the black dog would silently emerge from the mist. "Hold on to my fur," he'd tell James, "and I'll lead you to safety." But just as James reached out to touch the animal, the fog would close in and the dog would disappear. At this point James would wake up in terror.

The light clicked on and his mum came into the room with some water. "Have you had another nightmare?" she asked in concern. James nodded, gulping down the water greedily.

She sat down on the bed and brushed back his hair. "I've been thinking," she said. "I know you love dogs and I said you couldn't have one but ..." she sighed. "Perhaps you wouldn't keep having this nightmare if you had a dog of your own?"

James sat forward, brain whirring. "Oh, mum," he said.

"It's what I've always wanted."

"Hold on," she said. "There are conditions. If we get a dog from the kennels you must promise to look after it. Dogs aren't a five-minute wonder. You'll have to walk it, groom it and clean up after it. It'll be your responsibility. Think about it."

"I don't have to," said James, his eyes shining with excitement.

"Are you quite sure, James?" she said. But his grin told her he was. "OK, then, that's decided," said his mum. "We'll go to the kennels tomorrow."

The reception at the Blue Cross kennels turned out to be a concrete shed with a flat, corrugated roof. Inside, the lino was worn and scratched. Despite the smell of disinfectant, the pong of wet dog hung thickly in the air. The woman behind the desk introduced herself as Ruth. She had blonde hair tied in a ponytail and wore a baggy, green cardigan covered with animal hairs. "It's James, isn't it?" she said. "And you want a dog. Any particular type?"

James paused. He couldn't decide. There were little, wire-haired terriers with pert tails and bright eyes; long-haired Afghans with aristocratic noses; crinkly-eared spaniels with coats the colour of ginger biscuits. . .

"Well, let's go and see the animals," said Ruth sensing his problem. "Perhaps that will help you to make up your mind."

She took a huge ring of keys from a nail on the wall. James and his mum followed her to a terrace of kennels. Each had its own run with a fence around it. Ruth ran a key over the wire of the first one and a huge alsation bounded out, tail wagging, tongue out, bursting with curiosity. "This is Art," she said.

"He's very bright and very big. He needs a lot of exercise and gets bored easily. Most of all, he needs company, but that's true of all our dogs."

James crouched to be on a level with Art's head and the dog tried to lick him through the mesh. But Ruth had already moved on. The dogs, hearing they had visitors, came out of their kennels into their runs to see what the fuss was about.

But one run remained empty. Ruth ran a key along its fence. James stared beyond it into the door of the kennel. He thought he could just make out two eyes glinting in the gloom. "Why doesn't this dog come out like the rest?" he asked Ruth.

"He's very depressed," she said. "Some dogs miss their families more than others and labradors feel abandonment very deeply."

"What happened to him?" asked James.

"His family got him as a puppy for Christmas. He's a pedigree dog and they must have paid a great deal for him. But they didn't realise what it means to care for a dog or how much love and attention a dog needs. They claimed he kept knocking over their two small children.

"It's my guess," continued Ruth, "that they mistreated him. He may even have been hurt."

"Will he bite?" questioned James.

"No, he'd never bite anyone. He's big but gentle. Also, he's a dog with a broken heart and I've been hoping someone very special would come along and mend it for him. Now, why don't you go in and introduce yourself?" And she unlocked the gate in the fence.

James had to crouch low to get through the kennel's door. And when he adjusted to the darkness he saw a pair of sad brown eyes watching him intently from the corner.

"Oh boy, don't be sad," whispered James, crawling forward, willing the dog to trust him. He sat down on the straw in front of the animal who dropped his wide head onto his big paws. When James reached out to stroke the silky fur between the dog's ears he was upset to notice that the labrador flinched slightly. James kept his hand still for a while. "I won't hurt you," he said, beginning to stroke the dog's head again. He continued to reassure the animal in a quiet, soothing voice.

The dog, whose name was Jack, remained still. But although he wasn't moving, he could feel plenty. The ice in his heart melted with each stroke. For the first time in many lonely weeks Jack's big chest began to fill with hope. This boy has stayed longer than the rest, he thought. He touches me as if he wants to be my friend. He doesn't smell cruel. Do I dare look at him? Will he be disappointed and leave me?"

Summoning up all his courage, Jack slowly raised his big head from his paws and looked straight into the boy's eyes. And in them he saw all the love he had ever wanted or would ever need. The last piece of ice melted in his heart. His eyes smiled and his tail, still for so long, began to thump loudly on the straw. "You're the one," thought Jack. "Say you want me. Go outside and say you've chosen Jack the labrador. You won't be sorry."

"I have chosen you and I know I won't be sorry," said James to the dog's complete astonishment. "You're my dog now."

Jack's heart filled with such joy he felt he would burst his fur. The strength of his wagging tail sent straw flying over the kennel. "Now," said James, with a smile, "pull yourself together. Come and meet my mum."

Obediently Jack stood up, shook the straw from his sleek, black coat and trotted out into the winter sunlight behind James, his tail swinging like a pendulum. "This is our new dog," James yelled to his mum. "His name's Jack."

How very peculiar, thought Ruth, who had such a big lump in her throat she couldn't speak. I'm sure I never told the boy Jack's name.

■ CHAPTER TWO ■

FRIENDS AND ENEMIES

Jack loved living with James and his mum. He couldn't believe he had so much space to tear around in after the cramped kennels. He only saw James' mother get angry once. He had trampled over her flowerbeds to retrieve a ball. A scream went up from the kitchen. "Sit," she yelled in a very stern voice. And Jack did. She wagged a finger. "I love my garden so stay off the flowerbeds. And you," she said, pointing at James, "stop throwing the ball on my geraniums. You've ruined them." With that she stomped back inside.

What on earth are geraniums? thought Jack.

"Oh, they're those red flowers," said James. Jack was amazed. Was James one of those special human beings he'd heard about, the sort who are able to tune into a dog's mind? If so, he was a very lucky dog indeed.

Not everyone in the house had been pleased when he arrived. Fenella the cat was furious. How dare they bring a horrible, smelly, lolloping dog into the house, she thought. It was her domain, her territory. "Keep away from me, you vile creature," she spat at him during their first stand-off, back arched, her fur standing on end. "If you're going to live here, then I'll be off. And if you know what's good for you, you'll leave now." And after hissing and spitting and making a lunge towards Jack with a sharp claw, she made a dramatic exit through the catflap.

Fenella refused to return to the house for three days. However, she did eat every scrap of food they left in her bowl in the garden. When she eventually stopped sulking she made it clear to Jack that she would return only if he never tried to approach her. "Stay away from me and stay away from my food," she warned him, "otherwise I'll scratch your eyes out. There can be no question of us ever being friends."

The other person who resented Jack's arrival was Tom. He

was a stocky man with a black beard and a deep, booming voice. Whenever he visited the house the atmosphere changed. James' mum seemed to like him and he made her laugh. But James was always quieter than usual. Whenever Tom came round to dinner James would go to his bedroom afterwards to play on his computer taking Jack with him. He never stayed downstairs like he usually did to watch TV.

From his very first visit Tom acted as if Jack didn't exist, which puzzled the dog. He'd taken it for granted everyone loved him. Once he heard Tom tell James' mum: "He's a big, powerful dog and he'll need firm handling. I can't understand why you wanted an animal, it isn't as if you hadn't got enough on your plate." Jack didn't like the sound of that one little bit.

Once or twice Tom did stroke Jack after the dog came reluctantly wagging to greet him – but only when James' mum was looking. Jack knew Tom didn't really want to touch him and was just doing it to impress her. He didn't actually enjoy Tom stroking him. He had smelt something on his hands he never wanted to experience again – cruelty – and he trembled for the future. How could he protect James and his mum? How could he protect himself?

CHAPTER THREE

JACK'S SECRET

The chance to protect James came earlier than Jack thought but not in the way he expected. That Saturday he joined James and his friends on a trip to some open land called the heath where they had a den.

First they made sure their secret hideout could not be seen from the footpath. Then they headed for their favourite oak tree which had a hollow trunk and was great to climb. Watching them from below, Jack felt fed up and left out. He barked hoping to make them stop climbing higher. But all three boys yelled at him to shut up. Jack obeyed grumpily, then saw something which made him go tense with fear.

James was about to walk along a thick branch but Jack could see there was a deep crack underneath it. The wood which looked so solid was deadly. James' weight would send it crashing down. Jack whimpered. He barked furiously. He circled the tree in agitation but the boys only told him to shut up again.

"You're being bad, Jack," James shouted down at him. "Stop being so spoilt." And he put his knee on the branch. Jack barked louder, leaping again and again at the tree. But now James had two knees on the branch. And although it was against Dog Lore, even if he paid for it with his life, Jack knew what he must do.

Calmly, he sat at the foot of the tree and concentrated hard.

He felt himself flood with the forbidden sensation. The words bubbled up from deep inside making his head tingle. "Do not get on that branch. It's cracked and you could die," he said, in his head. He felt the power leave him.

As it travelled up the tree the trunk quivered. When the power reached James he gave a small jolt and look shocked. He stopped moving and looked down at Jack.

"What did you say?" he said. Jack repeated it. It came more easily the second time. The other two boys had heard nothing. They looked at each other and sniggered.

"What did you say, James?" jeered Kevin. "Are you talking to yourself? That's what weirdos do."

John, impatient, snapped at him: "Hurry up, James. You scared or something?"

But James edged back. "Don't go on the branch, it's cracked," he said in a shaky but determined voice.

"I can't see a crack," said Kevin, "you're just scared. Move over and let me have a go." He pushed past James, putting him off balance so he had to cling on to the trunk.

"It's so fat I could walk along it," boasted Kevin. He put a foot on the branch and raised his arms like a tightrope walker. But as he did they heard a great ripping crunch. The branch bent, broke and crashed to the ground. James and John managed to yank Kevin back at the last minute.

Kevin was shaking. "You saved my life," he stuttered to James, thinking of the terrible bang when the branch had hit the ground.

No, thought James, shaken himself but confused. It wasn't

me who saved Kevin, it was Jack my dog. But he said nothing.
He looked down at his loyal dog. He knew his friends would
never believe Jack had actually talked to him. But as
incredibly strange as it was, he knew he had.

The boys ambled downhill towards the road strangely silent,
and James told them he was taking Jack for one last run down
towards the lake. But as soon as they were alone, James sat
on the grass and confronted his dog.

"You spoke to me," James said. "I heard you. It was amazing." Jack pretended not to hear.

"Jack, please," said James. "You can't just leave it at that. I heard you talk, as if you were in my head."

Jack looked at James with his big, brown eyes and knew he could not lie, knew he would not get away with it.

"Yes," he said. "I did speak to you, James, but it's forbidden and I'm going to be in a lot of trouble. I did it because I was petrified you'd be hurt and I couldn't bear it."

James was amazed. "Why is it forbidden?" he said stroking Jack's head.

"It's against Dog Lore," said Jack solemnly. "If humans knew some of us could talk, just think what would happen. We'd be doing even more of your horrible jobs. And you'd use us in your silly wars and make us kill people. I might even end up in a factory, never able to smell the grass or go for walks. If you knew we could speak, life wouldn't be worth living."

"Can all dogs talk?" said James.

"No, very few of us. We have lost the bond with humans we once had when they depended so much on our hunting skills. There was a mutual respect then. I can do it because my mum and dad both possessed the power and I inherited it. They both had very good owners, who loved them. That helped."

"Why didn't John and Kevin hear you?" asked James.

"They're not close to me like you. I didn't have to try very hard. You have the rare gift of understanding animals. I knew that the first time I met you. I was so unhappy, my thoughts were scrambling around in my head, yet amazingly you knew my name was Jack."

"Ruth told me," said James.

"No she didn't," said Jack. "You tuned into my thoughts, I felt it as you stroked me." James thought back to the Blue Cross Kennels and the extraordinary closeness he had felt to Jack. He remembered how he so desperately wanted the dog to like him. Suddenly he realised he had found the dog who had appeared in his dreams, the dog who always came out of the mist to rescue him.

"Seriously, though," said Jack, licking a paw, "my talking must remain a secret between us. My elders will be furious with me and they have an uncanny way of finding out if anyone has acted against Dog Lore."

"What will they do to you?"

"I'll probably be summoned to see Canis, King of the Dogs," said Jack. "Because it's a first offence and I just about qualify as a puppy I may be let off with a supervision order."

"What does that mean?" said James.

"Well, every two weeks I'll have to present myself to Canis and swear I have spoken to no one but you and that you have sworn never to tell anyone. Can you do that, James? It will be so tempting to tell your friends you have a talking dog."

"I'll never tell anyone," said James. "But when will you have to see this Canis? Where does he live? How will you get to him?"

"Steady on," said Jack, "and I'll try to explain." Canis lives in a far away land and I've always known about him. All dogs do.

"When I was so unhappy in the kennels he told me a boy would come for me and say I was the dog of his dreams. That boy was you, James. You are my master now and I promise never to leave you and that I will always look after you."

What Jack didn't tell James was that Canis also told him he was a dog with a very special destiny. But to fulfil that destiny he would have to undergo three tests of courage. He had to triumph over water, evil and fire. "I believe you will succeed, Jack, for your heart is big," Canis said. Jack hadn't liked the sound of that one little bit and had tried to put it out of his mind. He did so again with a shake of his fur.

James was talking to him again. "Wow," he said. "I'd like to meet this Canis myself. Can I come with you to see him? Perhaps I could explain you had to speak to me to save my life."

Jack licked James' hand and looked up at him anxiously. "Please don't take offence," he said. "But I really don't think you can. I've never visited him in his own land and the journey may be dangerous. I don't know if a Human Being would even make it. Also, I feel that explaining myself to him is something I have to do on my own."

■ CHAPTER FOUR ■

KING OF THE DOGS

That night, deeply troubled, Jack finally fell asleep. Suddenly a warm breeze rippled through his fur, lifting his silky ears. The breeze became a strong wind. It raised him from his bed and carried him up through the roof of the house. He sped through the night towards a distant star. As he got nearer, Jack saw it was a giant catherine wheel. He hurtled through blue and green rings towards its blood-red centre. Terrified, Jack squeezed his eyes shut against the unbearable brightness. But just when he felt he could bear no more, he felt himself lowered gently to the ground. There was total silence. The wind gave his fur one last playful ripple, almost as if it was stroking him. And then it left. Jack was on his own. And he was scared.

Gingerly he opened one eye. Then, amazed, the other. He was lying by a stream on grass as soft as cotton wool. Beside him was a purple dog bowl full of milk. He lowered his head and gulped it down greedily. "Ahem," said a gruff voice behind him and Jack swizzled round in alarm. A boxer with a sleek brown coat and white chest was standing behind him.

"I'm Bruno, special adviser to Canis, King of the Dogs," continued the boxer. "He has requested that I escort you to his castle. Now, if you are quite rested, would you kindly follow me?" And without waiting for an answer he set off at a brisk pace across the grass towards a dark wood. "We are now entering The Forest Of a Thousand Sniffs," Bruno called over his shoulder. "The smells blow your mind if you're new to them. If you absolutely can't resist it I'm permitted to allow you two minutes writhing time. It'll help you feel at home."

The smells were driving Jack crazy. When they reached a part of the forest that smelt like very rare sirloin steak he could no longer resist the temptation. He rolled over onto his back, squirming left and right, paws in the air, coating the scent glands in his back with the delicious smell of prime meat, grunting with pleasure.

"Ok, Ok, that's quite enough," said Bruno, bored. Obediently Jack rose shakily to his feet and shook his head vigorously to clear it. Then he stumbled like a drunk after the boxer. But when he came to the end of the wood he tensed. In front of him him was a vast castle whose walls were made of sausages. Jack trotted after Bruno across a drawbridge into a courtyard. In the middle was an enormous kennel. When they were 10 metres away from it Bruno ordered Jack to sit. "You are now in Kennelworth Castle and this is as far as newcomers are allowed," he said. "Wait here." And he padded towards the kennel and disappeared through its gigantic door.

Jack looked around him then. Several dogs were lying nearby grooming, dozing and chewing bones. It all looked very relaxed. Then the air was rent by the loudest bark Jack had ever heard. It was so powerful that the trees shook. All the dogs dropped to the ground and lay their heads between their paws. Jack froze with fear.

"Get down, get down," whispered a little white West

Highland Terrier who had slithered over to him on her belly. "My name is Daisy, by the way," she said. "I'm chief consort to Canis, King of the Dogs, and I happen to know he wants to see you. When you are called, slither towards him on your belly and keep your eyes down. It's important to show respect and be obedient."

th was dry and his stomach had a large knot in
nd began to tremble. Jack, sneaking a look
through downcast eyes, saw a gigantic grey and white Old
English sheepdog. His two adornments were a huge gold
medallion round his neck which said: Best Of Breed: Crufts
1992 and a pair of shades.

The enormous dog moved forward and the earth shook
beneath his weight. Then he let out a bark as loud as thunder
while the dogs around him sank even lower. Canis, King of the
Dogs, surveyed them all, turning his massive head left and
right Then it swung back to face a cowering Jack.

"Come here," he boomed. Jack, his heart thumping,
slithered along the ground as Daisy had told him to do until he
was in the shadow of the giant sheepdog towering above him.

"So you CAN do as you're told, then" said Canis. He turned
to all the others. "You can all get up now," he said and then
looked down at the black labrador before him. "And you, too,
Jack. Let me look at you."

Jack's head jerked up ... and up ... and up, until he could
get a proper view of Canis's large head looming above him. He
could just about make out a pair of brown eyes under the
shaggy grey and white hair and shades but the experience was
intimidating. "You have a nice, shiny coat," said Canis
approvingly. "That means they're feeding you well. And you've
got expressive ears like your mother."

Jack wondered how Canis knew his mother but was afraid to
ask. "Oh, I knew her and your dad," said Canis. "He was a
magnificent animal, belonged to a lord who used him as a gun

dog. He was quite a catch. You come from very good stock, my boy. Anyway, that's enough history, how's life among the Human Beings?"

Jack was relieved. Canis hadn't brought up the talking thing, perhaps he didn't even know. "Well, sir, I had a bit of a bad start with that first family..."

"Not your fault, you were too good for them and they were too ignorant to know it," said Canis. "What about this new lot?"

"I now live with a boy called James and his mother. They're brilliant."

"Who's the Pack Leader in the house?"

Jack was puzzled, he'd never really considered that he was in a part-dog, part-human pack now.

"Let me put it another way," said Canis: "Who buys the food?"

"James' mum, sir."

"Well, then, that makes her the Pack Leader. Is she a good provider? Does the pack go hungry?"

"Oh no, sir. I'm very well cared for. And the Pack Leader even lets me sleep on James' bed with him."

"Any other Human Beings in the house?" asked Canis sternly.

"Well, there's this man who's the Pack Leader's boyfriend but he isn't there all the time."

Canis regarded him keenly. "You don't like him, I can tell. Why's that?"

"He doesn't like me. I don't think he likes dogs in general. He's always complaining that I smell and he mocks me when I eat. Although he hasn't hurt me I can smell cruelty on him."

The large circle of dogs that had noiselessly slithered forward to listen to the conversation emitted a low growl in unison.

"Hmmm," said Canis. "We don't like cruel." The dogs growled again. "Human Beings who are cruel to animals should be put down. Keep out of his way, son. If the Pack Leader is kind and wise she will find him out. Cruel people can't hide what they are and inevitably give themselves away by some petty act. Any other life forms in the house?"

"There's a cat, sir. She's called Fenella." The crowd of dogs started to howl and yelp like fury but Canis silenced them with one booming bark. "A cat," he said. "I asked you about life forms, not cats. They don't count for anything, horrible creatures. Has she spoken to you?"

"She has but only to tell me to stay away from her."

"Believe me, son, it's a rarity when a cat speaks to a dog. Perhaps she isn't quite so bad as some I've met. If the man doesn't like animals you and the cat may be able to put your mutual dislike aside to co-operate subtly in his downfall. Just a thought."

Canis made to move away and then abruptly turned and lay down in front of Jack and stared into his eyes. "Now Jack, I have a bone to pick with you," he said. Jack looked away, his heart sinking. So Canis did know about his talking and now he was for it. He furrowed his forehead trying to look humble.

"This James, he's become extremely special to you, hasn't he?" Jack nodded.

"So special that you have broken Dog Lore and spoken to him." Jack nodded again.

"And he understood you?"

Jack nodded for a third time, his heart heavy.

"You know that dogs should never let Human Beings know they can talk to them, don't you? You know what could happen to us. You can't trust them to have our interest at heart, only their own."

"But James would never...."

"I know, son. Usually Human Beings are too stupid to hear us when we talk. But this James has an open heart and obviously loves you."

"I love him too, sir. He'd never tell, not even his best friends. He said people would never believe him anyway and think he was mad. No one will find out."

Canis got up, paced a little and explained that some rare humans did have the gift of understanding dogs. "I belonged to one myself. She and I never told anyone about our special bond." He sighed heavily and continued: "Swear to me you will use your gift only to do good and promote happiness."

"I swear," said Jack solemnly, wondering if this meant he was off the hook.

He asked Canis if it was only human children who possessed the special gift of understanding dog speech.

"Yes, they tend to lose it as they get older and close off their imaginations," he said. "Now we've picked our little bone, Jack, it's time to send you back. Remember to avoid the man and the cat and love and protect James and the Pack Leader. Don't let me down. Now you must excuse me. I tire easily these days." And he headed back into the blackness of his kennel while the ground shook in time with his every stride.

■ **CHAPTER FIVE** ■

CRUELTY IN THE HOUSE

Tom was coming over once or twice a week. His visits made the Pack Leader happy but James and Jack were always careful to stay out of his way. Then James told Jack he and his mother had to go to a parents' evening at his school. Tom would be coming to the house to keep an eye on him.

"He says labradors can be destructive if they're left alone," said James. "Can you believe that?"

"He never misses a chance to rubbish me," said Jack. "I feel one of my depressions coming on." He hoped Tom wouldn't eat in front of him. He never gave Jack leftovers like James and the Pack Leader. And he'd always smile slyly at him as he shovelled his uneaten food into the bin. Jack lay his head on James' lap practising being fed up for later.

Tom hadn't arrived by the time they had to go. The Pack Leader looked at her watch in irritation and said: "We can't leave it any longer. He can let himself in." She left a plate of chicken casserole on the kitchen work surface for Tom to microwave. Fenella, feigning sleep on her cushion near the back door, opened an eye and smirked. Her tummy rumbled in anticipation.

As soon as the front door slammed behind James and his mum, Fenella stretched and vaulted on to the work surface where she walked up to the plate, whiskers quivering. "Oh yummy, it's bird. My favourite," she said. "Pity it's not raw

but you can't have everything," and she crouched down and swallowed a huge piece of meat. Jack was worried. It was Tom's food and there was bound to be trouble. He heard a car approach and although Fenella had warned him never to talk to her he felt he must.

"Fenella," said Jack." I know you don't speak to me but I heard a car ..."

"Oh do stop spoiling my delicious chicken dinner," taunted Fenella. "If she'd left it on the floor you would have gobbled it up. Stop pretending you have more control." She narrowed her eyes at Jack, then calmly carried on eating. Jack felt there was nothing more he could do so he went and lay by the front door. It was the last place he'd seen James and his mum and the first place he'd see them again. The key turned, Jack stiffened and Tom let himself in, cursing when he almost tripped over Jack.

"Blasted dog," he said in answer to Jack's half-hearted welcoming wag. Jack hoped this had given Fenella enough time to get off the work surface. But when Tom strode into the kitchen he knew his ploy had failed because Tom let out a bellow of rage.

"Wretched cat," he yelled. "I'll teach you to eat my dinner, you vile creature." Jack, who had followed Tom, saw him lurch towards Fenella who was so startled she was wide-eyed and rooted to the spot. She had a telltale piece of chicken hanging from one side of her mouth. Tom took Fenella by the scruff of her neck and hurled her across the kitchen so hard she hit the wall. The dazed cat picked herself up but, instead of fleeing, she cowered as Tom advanced upon her. Jack feared he was going to kick her. Without thinking he let out a low, menacing growl.

Tom turned on him. "You spoilt, overweight excuse of a dog," he fumed "How dare you growl at me. It will be the last noise you ever make."

And he took hold of the loose skin on Jack's neck and dragged him through the house to the patio doors that led to the back garden. Seeing her chance, Fenella gathered her wits and jumped through the catflap.

When he got the patio doors open, Tom kicked Jack in the rump to force him into the garden. Jack gave a yelp of pain. "Plenty more where that came from," said Tom sneering. "I am the master in this house, not you. And you'd do well to remember it. No more bed, no more sofa, just the cold night. Try being a real dog." And he slammed the doors shut and pulled the curtains so he could no longer see Jack outside.

Booted out in the cold, the cat and the dog stayed a good two metres apart: he on the ground licking the place where Tom had kicked him, she on the wall of the raised flowerbed above. Fenella began to groom herself, licking a paw and rolling it over her head.

"Why don't you like me?" said Jack at last. "I mean, what is it you don't like about me?"

Fenella sighed. "Now where do I start?" she purred sarcastically. "Well, for a start, you bolt your food, then get your nose right in your bowl. Sometimes you chase it all over the floor and don't notice I'm in the way."

"That's how all dogs eat," said Jack.

"Quite," said Fenella. "You're disgusting animals. You don't even bother to wash yourselves after a meal."

"We don't need to," said Jack. "And I don't see what's so great about putting all that cat food smell from your saliva all over your fur as you're doing now."

"If cat food's so nasty and smelly why do you spend so much time trying to eat it from my bowl when you think I'm not looking," retorted Fenella.

Jack had no reply. It was horribly true.

"Another thing," said Fenella. He waited. There was more? "You've no grace, no elegance. You dogs bump into things, knock things over with your wagging tails."

"At least I can express happiness," said Jack huffily.

"We purr - and purrs don't break vases," said Fenella.

"They are a deeply irritating noise," snapped Jack.

"Not as irritating as that ridiculous display of dog machismo known as barking. And it's not only your bad manners and lack of grace I can't stand but the fact that you are all such crawlers – you do everything Human Beings want. I don't know how you can have any self-respect. And you have no independence from them. Me, for instance, I'm going out for the evening now. There's a cats' chorus rehearsal over near the river."

"You actually rehearse to make that vile sound?" said Jack.

"Oh, you're so ignorant. Do you know how difficult it is to sing just a slightly different note from your neighbour? Do you realise what breath control is necessary to sustain a really meaningful caterwaul? Of course you don't ... I don't even know why I'm trying to explain. Anyway, after rehearsal, myself and my friend Miss E. Perkins will be hungry so we'll go and kill something small and furry. When my evening is finished and I'm tired I can let myself back into the house through the catflap. You, on the other hand, must pathetically wait here until a Human Being takes pity on you and lets you in."

Jack's rump was throbbing with pain where Tom had kicked him. He stared at his paws trying not to give in to self-pity. Fenella was right, he had to stay outside. And he knew Tom would deliberately leave him in the garden until James came back. Tom did not know, of course, that Jack could tell his young master what had happened. But he decided not to do that. James would be so angry and dislike Tom even more.

"Well I'll be off then," said Fenella. She sighed heavily. "This is difficult," she began, "but thank you for that growl. It stopped Tom kicking me. I'm extremely grateful. And we cats honour our debts. I owe you, Jack. And I'm sorry you got punished." And, with that, Fenella leapt onto the fence and was swallowed up by the night. Jack lay on the cold concrete patio, his head on his paws. But Fenella's praise had made him warm inside. He decided he might as well doze off while he waited for James to come home.

But Jack's determination to remain silent about his cruel treatment was sabotaged by the pain in his rump. Jack found it difficult to get on the bed that night. When James tried to push him up he yelped in pain. "What's wrong, Jack? Are you injured?"

asked James. "You haven't been hit by a car, have you?"

"No," said Jack. "Anyway, it's just a bruise. Stop making a fuss. I can't even remember how it happened. Nothing's broken."

"You don't know that," said James. "Mum and I will get you checked out by the vet just in case."

"But I hate going to the vet," said Jack.

"Tough," said James, "you'll just have to put up with it. Anyway we've never taken you to our vet. I haven't met him myself. You're the first pet I've ever had."

"Well, it'll be a first if I do like a vet," retorted Jack grumpily.

Next day, James and the Pack Leader bundled the reluctant dog into the car. The vet's name was Nick and after he had examined Jack he confirmed the dog was badly bruised.

He turned to James. "Would you mind taking Jack outside for a moment while I have a private word with your mother?" he asked.

In the waiting room the boy and the dog strained their ears but Nick's voice was annoyingly soft. All of a sudden the Pack Leader exclaimed loudly: "No one in our house would do that. It's unthinkable." There was more whispering. Then she emerged looking upset. Nick the vet looked ill at ease.

"What did the vet want to speak to you about, mum?" said James when they were in the car.

"If you must know," said The Pack Leader, "he asked if anyone had kicked Jack. I told him it was out of the question."

"I hope he didn't think it was me," said James horrified.

"If he did, he doesn't now," said the Pack Leader. "Anyway he's just doing his job. He was very thorough."

But James was deep in thought. Suddenly he realised who could have kicked Jack. He could have screamed with fury. It was Tom. It had to be Tom.

As soon as they were alone in James' bedroom he rounded on Jack. "It's no good lying," he said, "Tom kicked you, didn't he?" Jack looked miserable. "Tell me," said James. "Tell me so I can make sure he doesn't hurt you again." Jack reluctantly described what had happened while he and his mother had been out. James felt sick with rage. "I want to kill him," he exploded. "That cruel, horrible pig."

"You'll do nothing," said Jack. "The only way you could know what Tom did is if I'd told you. And you promised you would never let anyone know I could speak. Obviously he doesn't like animals but because your mum does, he puts on an act in front of her."

"He'll slip up sooner or later, then we'll see how much she likes him," said James. "We'll get him. Just you wait and see."

■ CHAPTER SIX ■

THE FIRST TEST

James did his best to ignore Tom. Then one warm spring day he took Jack to the river with his friends. When they stopped on the bridge to watch the ducks, Jack found the gaze of four goats in a nearby paddock very threatening. He barked at them but they just continued to stare and chew. When he bounded off he heard them laughing. "Come back and scare us some more," taunted the biggest goat, collapsing on the straw, helpless with mirth. "We've seen off a troll. You're nothing."

"I'm coming back later, then I'll show you," boasted Jack trying to catch up with the boys with the sound of goat guffaws ringing in his ears. Goats are even worse than cats, he thought.

The boys stopped again. They threw sticks in the water for Jack to retrieve and then decided to build a dam. Bored, Jack wandered along the footpath and saw a little girl picking daisies on the river bank. Her mother was looking at a bird's nest high in the trees through binoculars.

"Don't go out of my sight," the woman told the girl. "The river bank is steep here and you might fall in." But her warning came too late. There was a sudden shrill scream followed by a splash. The child was in the water.

"Oh my God, my daughter can't swim and nor can I," screamed the terrified woman. "Help someone, help." But help was already on its way. Jack had hurled himself into the river and was swimming determinedly towards the little girl.

She was spluttering and yelling as the current took her further from the bank. "Mum," she cried, before her head disappeared beneath the water. She came up thrashing and choking but Jack had reached her. The frightened child fastened her hands round his neck, digging her fingers into his fur so hard Jack cried in pain. He could hardly breathe and he found it difficult to swim with her added weight. His head kept going under the water. On the bank the woman kept pace with him. She was calling for help on her mobile phone.

Jack felt as if his lungs would burst. But just when he felt he could go on no longer, he rounded a bend and saw the boys.

Kevin spotted the labrador first. "Jack's got a child on his back," he said. "He keeps going under. We must help him!"

All three boys splashed towards Jack until the water was up to their chests. As the dog drew level with them, they caught hold of his collar and tugged him towards the shallows. A man waded out to help. James saw with some embarrassment that it was Nick the vet who handed the child to her mother.

When he reached the bank Jack slumped on the grass, shut his eyes and began to snore. Nick gently felt the dog's throat. "He's a bit bruised," he told James, " but I don't think there's any lasting damage."

"You're a brave dog," said James stroking Jack's head. Nick watched for a minute. "There's something I'd like to clear up with you, James," he said. "Your mum probably told you what I said to her at the surgery."

James nodded.

"I didn't mean to suggest you had hurt Jack. You probably hated me for saying it." James said nothing.

Nick continued: "But it was such an odd place for a dog to be hit by a car. Jack can't tell us what happened so I have to try to find out. Sometimes I get things wrong." James bit his lip, remembering the promise he'd made to his dog.

"That's OK," he said eventually. "I understand."

"I'll call round and look at Jack's throat in a few days, if that's all right. There'll be no charge."

James smiled. "That'd be great," he said.

A policeman came over to talk to them.

"This is my brother Dennis," said Nick.

"You must be very proud of your dog," said Dennis. "He save that child's life. Her mother has told me about it."

The boys woke Jack and slowly walked back to the lane. This time the goats did not laugh at Jack. One even trotted over. "We heard what you did. Respect," he said. Jack nodded, too tired to reply but pleased all the same.

But when James' mother arrived in the car she blew a fuse when she saw the soaking boys and dog. They had no chance to explain. Jack, looking out of the car window, was confused. Had he done good or bad? He did wonder if he'd just undergone the ordeal by water that Canis had warned him about. Had he passed that first test of courage? He hoped the other two tests about evil and fire wouldn't be so hard. He wished he knew why he had to do them in the first place.

He'd tried asking other dogs on the heath what destiny meant and what the three tests were but they didn't know what he was talking about. Only one elderly pug seemed to understand. "Oh, yes," he said. "The three dreaded tests to fulfil your destiny. I was told about them. I tried my best but I turned out to be a bit of a failure. My heart wasn't big enough." Jack tried to question him further but he was on a lead and his owner yanked him away.

The Pack Leader carried on ranting until they got home. A reporter and a photographer from the local paper were waiting on the doorstep. Only then did the boys get a chance to tell their story. The neighbours came out of their houses and wanted to know what had happened.

The only thing to spoil the day was Tom. He pushed his way through the small crowd to lay claim on the Pack Leader. And he was particularly put out when the paper didn't want a picture of him.

"Surplus to requirements as usual," Jack heard him hiss to her. "I'll be indoors when you've all stopped making a show of yourselves." And shooting a look of pure venom at Jack, he stalked off.

News of Jack's heroism quickly spread. The next day a TV camcrew came round to film them all. They were to be on television that very night.

The boys tore round to Kevin's house for the evening. James had really wanted to stay home with his mum and watch himself on TV, but Tom was there and he may have spoilt it for them with his bad mood.

Seeing themselves on TV was such a thrill, even though it was over in a flash. Even Nick the vet was interviewed and spoke glowingly of Jack's bravery. "He's a nice looking young man," said Kev's mum.

"She's always on the lookout for someone nice for your mother," laughed Kev.

"I'm not," said his mum indignantly. "Anyway she's got that Tom now."

Silence greeted her remark. As the boys exchanged glances Kev's mum realised James did not like Tom. She wondered why.

When James arrived home later he was surprised to find his mother alone.

"Tom had to go," she said in a flat voice. "But I saw the programme. It was great." James wondered if she and Tom had rowed. Perhaps she was at last beginning to believe he was not as nice as he pretended to be.

James enjoyed several Tom-free days after that and when he heard he was coming round on Friday decided to spend the evening at Kevin's house. Later that night, when he quietly let himself in by the kitchen door, he could hear his mum and Tom talking in the sitting room. He couldn't resist listening. He heard his mother say: "You behaved like a jealous child. Because you weren't the centre of attention you sulked and tried to spoil it for me and James."

"Don't you think your precious son is too big for his boots already?" hissed Tom. "Now he's been on tele there'll be no holding him. He's been too long without a father and you've allowed him to do as he pleases."

"That's not true," retorted the Pack Leader. "But you're right on one count. He is my precious son and don't you ever underestimate how much he means to me."

"Oh please, let's change the subject," said Tom, "before I'm sick."

James was furious. He wants my mum, he thought savagely, but he certainly doesn't want me. What am I going to do?

He heard the rustle of someone leaving the sofa so he quickly retraced his steps to the kitchen. Noisily, he slammed the door as if he had just arrived. "I'm home," he shouted.

■ CHAPTER SEVEN ■

NEW DAD CRISIS

James and the Pack Leader sat lounging on the sofa, the dog stretched across their laps. Every so often Jack would twitch and give little yelps and James wondered what he was dreaming about.

Suddenly the Pack Leader said to James: "You do like Tom, don't you?"

James momentarily stopped stroking Jack and wondered what was coming next. Jack, suddenly alert and sensing trouble, opened his eyes.

"Only," said the Pack Leader, "he's spending a lot of time round here now and it seems silly to keep paying for two houses and two sets of bills...."

James was way ahead of her. He did not want the conversation to go on to its appalling but inevitable conclusion. He sat staring at the television but could think of absolutely nothing to say.

"You and Tom seem to get on OK," said his mother. James looked down and saw Jack, now fully awake, furrow his brow in sympathy.

"Are you listening, James?" said his mother. "This is important."

"Yes mum, I'm listening," said James in his most irritable voice.

"Well, I know you've had me all to yourself for a long time.

Having someone else here would need a lot of adjustments on all our parts but how would you feel if Tom moved in permanently?"

James' stomach lurched. "Sick," he wanted to say but he loved his mum and didn't want to hurt her. He could see that Tom made her happy but she had no idea how spiteful he had been to the pets when she wasn't around. And after overhearing his nasty comments about him, James knew the man regarded him as a spoilt brat. Although Tom had never been physically aggressive towards him he often looked as if he wanted to be. Tom was always complaining about the mess James made, always telling him off for something trivial. There was tension in the house whenever Tom was there. Although James tried hard to be on his best behaviour it never seemed good enough.

James remembered when Tom had come home one night when his mum was out and found Jack on the sofa with him.

"Dogs on the furniture – I've seen everything now," fumed Tom, throwing down his newspaper, his voice shaking with anger. "Make that dirty animal sit on the floor where he belongs." Without thinking, James had snapped back: "Jack's not dirty and it isn't your sofa. It's my mum's and she lets him sit on it." Tom's eyes had narrowed and their pupils became little blackcurrants of hatred. "We'll see about that," he said, jutting his jaw at James.

Later the Pack Leader had suggested James keep Jack off the sofa when Tom was alone with them to "keep the peace". James had come near to hating her for taking Tom's side against him and Jack. He spent the rest of the evening sulking in his bedroom.

James pulled himself back to the present. His mother was still speaking. "So what do you think?" she said. "Would you like a new dad?"

James' stomach lurched. No, he most certainly did not want Tom as his new dad. He was not going to let his mother fool herself that she was doing this for him. She was doing it for herself.

"Look mum," he said, keeping his eyes fixed on the TV, though he had no idea what he was watching, "it's your life and you can do what you want. Whatever makes you happy."

"But will it make you happy?" she asked.

"I'm happy the way things are," said James. He'd had enough of the conversation. He wanted it to stop in case he blurted out the truth. And the truth was that he hated Tom for the harm he had done to his dog. He never wanted to see him again as long as he lived. But instead of saying any of that he said: "Can I change channels, only they're showing Red Dwarf repeats on the other side?"

The Pack Leader sighed. "Do what you want," she said heavily and left the room.

James looked down at his dog. He was completely miserable. Jack, feeling his despair, pressed his wet nose into the boy's palm.

"Try not to worry," Jack told him. "I'll find a way to stop that man moving in here and ruining our lives. The Pack Leader is a good person but she's just gone a bit crazy. Tom treats her well, makes her laugh a lot, takes her out, buys her presents, it's no wonder she's smitten. You can't blame her for trying to find love because that's what all human adults do."

"But she's got all my love," said James. "I don't want that man here. He won't make any of us happy, including her. He's a two-faced phoney. She never sees his nasty side. He's hurt you and Fenella and I'm frightened of him." Jack sat up, put a paw on James' shoulder and looked at him with worried brown eyes. "She'll just have to witness his spite and that will make her feel differently about him," he said. "And then we'll have to find her a man that we both like so she won't be lonely."

"Oh, is that all?" said James sarcastically.

"Trust me," said Jack. "I'll take advice."

"Are you going to see Canis again?" said James.

"Yes. He's the wisest dog in the world. Perhaps he'll have a plan."

JACK: KING OF THE DOGS

■ CHAPTER EIGHT ■

LEGAL BEAGLES

That night Jack whizzed through the sky to the centre of the catherine wheel. He landed on the cotton wool grass by the stream and Bruno escorted him through the Forest of a Thousand Sniffs to Kennelworth Castle.

Canis could not receive them immediately because he was sleeping. Daisy fetched Jack some sausages and milk and sat with him while he waited. "How did Canis get to be king?" he asked her.

Daisy sighed. "You have to understand he is one of a long line of our monarchs. They all adopt the name Canis when they are chosen, according to Dog Lore. Being king is an exhausting job," she continued. "My Canis has had the title for some years and it's beginning to take its toll. His brain's as sharp as ever but because of his increasing size he needs more and more sleep."

"Do you mean he could become even bigger than he is now?" said Jack, amazed.

"Most probably," said Daisy. "You see, a dog literally has to grow into the job. He's normal size when he starts but as soon as he becomes king he grows and grows as he shoulders more responsibility. That's why any dog chosen has to have a big heart to start with, otherwise the weight gain would kill him.

"My Canis will gradually return to normal size when he steps down as king. He and I will resume the lives we had

before he was chosen. He'll just be plain old Digby again. Believe it or not, many of the dogs around you have been king. The last one was Bruno, who is now special adviser."

"How is a successor chosen?" asked Jack.

"We all get a vote," said Daisy. "Usually it's obvious who should be king so there's never a real contest."

"Why is it so obvious?"

"Very few dogs could do it. As well as having a big heart to cope with the physical demands of the job they have to pass the three tests you've heard about. They must triumph over water, evil and fire. Basically they have to be willing to lay down their lives for their master or mistress."

"That's a lot to ask of a dog." said Jack. He felt a bit uneasy.

"Yes. Now you see why it's so difficult to find the next king. There's also a deeper reason for insisting why a new King of the Dogs must prove his absolute loyalty to mankind."

Daisy explained that now they had supermarkets, humans rarely needed their dogs to help them hunt for food.

Dogs once alerted their masters enemies were approaching by barking. Now Human Beings had burglar alarms. "The one thing we can still provide for them is our absolute loyalty in an increasingly treacherous world," said Daisy. "So long as we love them as only a dog can, we have a chance of surviving as a species. We can still be of use.

"When a dog performs the ultimate act of heroism for a Human Being – laying down his life – it makes them remember why they love us, too."

"It's a shame Human Beings aren't prepared to die for us like that," said Jack. "It's a bit of an unequal relationship. I know where the term 'underdog' comes from now."

Daisy laughed. "You're right, Jack. But we can't hope to change the world that much, only to make it more bearable for all of us.

"And being Canis is not quite so terrible as I've described it. If we think a dog is potential king material we invite him up here a few times so we can look him over. Then he knows that if he does lose his life there's something wonderful waiting beyond it. And now I've said far too much."

The ground shook. Canis was stirring. The huge dog emerged from his kennel and advanced towards Daisy and Jack. "I don't remember calling for you," he said, eyeing the labrador suspiciously. "I hope you have a very good reason for coming here and disturbing me."

Jack gulped. "I'm truly sorry, sir, but I need your help," he began.

"That man Tom is disturbing the peace of mind of my master, James. He is the Pack Leader's boyfriend, if you remember. Now she wants him to move in. James is frightened of him and so am I and the cat. We want to know what we can do to stop this happening."

Canis peered down at Jack from his great height and shook his shaggy head. "I don't think you can take any action legally," he said. "If you interfered in human relationships you would be in breach of Dog Lore. But there might be a way. We'll have to consult the Legal Beagles."

Canis let out two enormous barks that made a small tree tremble. The longer, even louder one that followed, felled it. Within seconds five beagles strode into the clearing on their short legs. Each one carried a heavy scroll tied with a red ribbon in his mouth. Canis explained Jack's problem. They sat down in a ring, unfurled their scrolls and pored over them with great concentration and lots of dribbling. "They are looking at previous cases to see if a similar situation has been dealt with before," said Canis. "The main thing is to avoid breaching Dog Lore."

"Actually," said Jack, "no one has really explained Dog Lore to me properly. What is it?"

The beagles raised their eyes and sighed heavily. Then one stepped forward and cleared his throat. "Dog Lore," he explained, "is the canine equivalent of the 10 commandments which all dogs obey so they and Human Beings can live in peace. The laws are:

1. I will lay down my life for my master.
2. I will give my master absolute loyalty.
3. I will never let Human Beings know I can talk.
4. I will never bite a Human Being.
5. I will honour the Pack Leader because they provide the food.
6. I will allow myself to be taken to the vets no matter how scared I am.
7. I will never steal another dog's bone.
8. I will bark at postmen or dustmen approaching my master's home.
9. I will despise cats because they despise me.
10. I will not interfere in human relationships because they are impossible to understand anyway."

"Well," said Jack brightening up. "I'm within Dog Lore on a couple of counts. I'm being loyal to my master and I'm honouring the Pack Leader by trying to get rid of a man who is unworthy of her."

"Ah," said the head beagle, raising his doleful eyes in irritation, "that's just your judgment. Perhaps she believes this Tom is worthy of her. If you interfere, you risk her turning against you. That means you could end up with no food in your bowl. Your master would be like a bone pulled and pushed between the two of you. I'm afraid there are some aspects of human relationships us dogs will never understand. We must keep out of them for the greater good."

Jack put his head on his paws, depressed. "I promised James I would help," he said. "I can't let him down."

"You had no right to make a promise you couldn't keep," said Canis. "You have much to learn. However, I'm not entirely displeased with you. You endured your ordeal by water bravely – the first of the three important tests. I am proud of you."

Jack should have been pleased but talking about the three tests always frightened him. He didn't want to be reminded he still had two more to do. He didn't like the idea at all. Rescuing the little girl had been bad enough. He still had evil and fire to come. He may have done well so far but Canis had told him off very badly over the Tom thing. He was still upset about that.

Daisy trotted over and put a little white paw on Jack's head. She nuzzled his ear and tried to lighten his mood. "No one would deny you tried to act for the best by volunteering to try to do something about Tom," she said. "You just lack experience. I'm afraid you'll learn, like we all do, that sometimes we have to endure situations that we're powerless to change. However, things do have a way of working out, even if you do nothing."

"I wish I believed that," said Jack grumpily.

"You must believe it," said Daisy a trifle sharply. "You'll just have to trust this Pack Leader to do the right thing for her pack in her own time." Behind her, the Legal Beagles nodded in agreement while furling up their scrolls.

"All you have to do is wait," continued Daisy. "I know it's hard for a young, impatient puppy but it's the best advice I can give and I suggest you take it."

And she trotted back to Canis who looked down at her fondly. "She's right." he told Jack. "Daisy's small but she possesses an awesome wisdom. I suggest you take her advice on board."

Jack realised the advice was good. But he'd thought if Canis could help him get rid of Tom it would be best for everyone. He'd counted on that help. He was also worried about the other two tests. What happened if he wasn't up to them? What if his heart wasn't big enough and things went wrong? What would happen to him then?

■ CHAPTER NINE ■

THE SECOND TEST

Tom moved in and James was miserable. Tom was especially grumpy when he found Nick the vet in the house sharing a cup of tea with him and his mum. After Nick had examined Jack's bruised throat he had told them about his big ginger tom cat called McCarthy. Fenella, listening in as usual, had jumped on to his lap.

"What a cosy scene," said Tom acidly. Nick, feeling unwelcome, left soon after.

James tried hard to be nice to Tom. But the better he behaved the more the man seemed to hate him. Then, to James' dismay, his mother said she was meeting a friend for lunch in London that Saturday and Tom would again be in charge. After the last experience James decided the best tactic would be to go to the heath for the day with Kev and John. But on the day Tom had very different ideas.

"I think you should tidy that tip of a bedroom of yours and surprise your mother," said Tom rubbing his hands. "It's a disgrace and it stinks of dog." And with this he cast a withering glance at Jack.

"But I've made arrangements to go over the heath with my friends," protested James.

"Well unmake them," snarled Tom. "Your room is to be tidied, polished and vacuumed and then perhaps it won't stink so much. You never seem to do anything to help other people, perhaps it's time you learned."

James flushed with anger. He clenched his fists so hard his nails bit into his palms. But with every bit of willpower he possessed he said nothing.

He was determined not to give Tom an excuse to punish him. Jack whispered: "Well done. Don't take him on – it's what he wants."

James stomped upstairs. His room didn't look too bad. If he put on a bit of speed he could tidy it and still get to the heath with his friends. He crammed clothes in drawers, stuffed things under the bed and vacuumed and polished. Then he heard the front door go and sprinted downstairs. He was just in time to hear Tom tell Kev and John: "He won't be coming out today. Sorry boys, perhaps another time." James watched in disbelief as Tom slammed the door on them.

"But I've finished my room," he said.

Tom turned on him. "In half an hour? The state it was in? I don't think so. Show me." Heavily James climbed the stairs with Jack in tow and opened his bedroom door knowing Tom would find fault with his efforts. He wasn't wrong. Tom immediately discovered all the stuff James had hidden under the bed. He threw it into the centre of the room in a big heap. Then he began opening drawers and tipping them out, adding them to the pile. It now looked much more untidy than it had before James started.

"Call that tidy?" yelled Tom. "If you fold things neatly in your drawers there'll be room for everything without chucking it under the bed. Your poor mother."

"I hate him," said James, kicking the pile after Tom had

marched downstairs. "He's a mean, spiteful, nasty pig."

"He may be all of those things," said Jack, "but he's in charge. You'll have to do what he wants."

So James did. The sun was beating down outside making the room stuffy and hot. But James with murder in his heart and tears of frustration in his eyes waded though the huge pile. He sorted, folded and put rubbish in black bin liners. When the heap had been disposed of he turned to Jack and said: "There's nothing a reasonable person could find wrong with this. But he's not reasonable and I don't intend to give him the chance. We can let ourselves out. Let's join Kev and John on the heath. By the time we come back, mum'll be home and he won't be able to be nasty to me any more."

"It's a good plan," said Jack guardedly, "but why don't we just stay here – just for today? Tom doesn't give a fig how tidy your bedroom is. He just wants to stop you having fun and show you who's boss. If he catches you sneaking out he'll think you have defied him and he'll be furious."

"He won't catch us," said James. "Why should I have to spend a beautiful day like this indoors? Mum would never make me stay in. Won't you come with me?"

"Of course I will," said Jack. "But I'm trying to protect you."

"I don't need it," said James. "Follow me." James eased open the bedroom door and tiptoed across the landing. They could hear the football commentary from the TV in the sitting room and James thought Tom was watching it. He may have even dozed off. "Coast clear," James whispered to Jack. They made their way downstairs, treading particularly lightly on the bits that creaked.

Despite their efforts, one floorboard made a loud groan and they paused, still as statues. James grimaced. He held his breath but the sitting room door remained shut and they continued their descent. At last James reached the front door. He was just slowly and noiselessly turning the handle when a voice thundered behind him: "Where DO you think you are going?"

"Out," said James bravely turning to face Tom. "Over the heath as I planned."

"But I said you would not be going out," said Tom advancing towards the dog and boy from the kitchen where he had been concealed. James cursed his stupidity. It had not been the TV in the sitting room he could hear but the much nearer kitchen radio.

"Look," he told Tom, "I've done everything you've asked." He tried to sound calm and reasonable. But his heart was thumping its way through his chest and Jack had pressed his bulk against his leg for moral support.

"But I said you were NOT to go out. What don't you understand? Are you thick or something?"

James could control his anger no longer.

"You're not my dad, you've got no right to keep me in against my will, you spiteful bully."

Tom's eyes bulged with icy hatred.,

"No right," he bellowed. "We'll see about rights," and he drew back a large, hairy hand aiming to grab James' collar and frogmarch him back upstairs. But James ducked to one side and Tom's hand crashed into the door frame.

"You little so and so," bellowed Tom, furious. "That really hurt." His hand shot out again and James, thinking Tom was going to hit him this time, tried to escape. But he tripped over Jack at his feet. He fell hard against the post at the bottom of the stairs and blood began to stream from his nose.

"I've had about as much of you as I can take, you spoilt brat," hissed Tom moving to lean over James. Jack, fearing his master was going to be hurt, could finally take no more.

With a menacing growl he leapt at Tom's arm and fastened his teeth round it. Tom's eyes widened in fright and pain. The huge teeth sank into his flesh as the dog bit harder. Tom stumbled backwards crying in agony, unable to push Jack away. Then Jack let go and fell to the ground. But he stood between Tom and James baring his teeth, snapping and growling. Tom backed off, scared and holding his arm. Jack had broken his skin with the bite and blood had seeped though on to his shirt.

With chilling fury he surveyed James and Jack. "Well, you've done it now," he said. "You and your precious dog. I'm going to get into my car, drive to the hospital and get a tetanus jab and my arm bandaged. Do you know what they do with dogs who assault people? Do you want me to tell you? They put them down. That is a polite way of saying that they kill them. When your mother finds out she's got a dog who bites people she will take him to that vet you like so much. He will give Jack an injection to put him to sleep permanently. She won't want to share a house with a vicious dog who might turn on her if he feels like it." And picking up his car keys from the hall table he left the house slamming the door behind him.

James, holding a tissue to his bleeding nose, threw his arms around Jack's neck. "Oh Jack, I'm sorry, it's all my fault," he said. "All you did was defend me. I couldn't live without you and I don't intend to. Come on, we're getting out of here."

Jack, still shocked that he had actually bitten a Human Being in anger, watched as James stuffed his sports bag full of food from the fridge and cupboards. He took some dog tins and mixer for him, too, and hefted down his sleeping bag from the airing cupboard. "Come on, boy," he said. "We're going into hiding. There's no way I could ever let anything happen to you."

James, his head down, and Jack, with his tail between his legs, left the house and headed towards the heath. Fenella, who had witnessed everything sat gazing after them from the kitchen windowsill. "They haven't a cat in hell's chance of surviving in the wild," she thought. "I expect I'll have to help them."

■ CHAPTER TEN ■

SLEEPING ROUGH

Fenella shadowed them all the way to the heath, darting behind bushes and tiptoeing across front gardens. Naturally nosey and secretive, she had often spied on James and his friends and guessed his destination. He'll go to his den, she thought. How stupid. It would be the first place anyone would look for them.

When James arrived at the den he was dismayed to find his friends had already left. He began to feel incredibly alone. Rifling through a few old tins where conkers, marbles and various finds were kept, he discovered a couple of chocolate biscuits. But he didn't feel like eating them. By then, he, too, realised the den would not be a safe hiding place. When he didn't come home his mum would question Kev and John and discover where it was.

Jack took himself off for a snuffle. The ground always smelt particularly good in the early evening. Smells helped him think. He heard an urgent hiss from behind a bush and raised his head. There sat Fenella, bolt upright, her tail curled round her front paws.

"You can't stay in that den," she told him.

"Where else can we go?" said Jack.

"I know a special hiding place," said Fenella. "It's a hollow piece of bank under a fallen tree root. Because it's in a dip it's below the main footpath so no one can see it."

"Thank you," said Jack, "but we won't be able to hide for ever. The Pack Leader will be frantic when she finds James has gone. Tom will tell her I've bitten him and the police will be called to search for us. When they find me I will be put down. Although I'm trying so hard to be brave I tremble every time I think about it."

"I'm not surprised," said Fenella. "I saw everything and I know you were only trying to protect James from that monster. Look, I'll wait here. Tell James about the hiding place. Then you can both follow me."

James was amazed when Jack explained about Fenella. "I didn't know she could talk," he said. "What remarkable pets I have."

"Oh she can't talk to humans like I can," said Jack airily not wishing James to regard Fenella as highly as him. "Normally cats don't even speak to dogs on principle. But I did her a favour when I stopped Tom kicking her. And she does care very much about you and wants to help."

Fenella's hideaway turned out to be well concealed. They had to fight their way through ropes of ivy and brambles to find it. The floor of the hollow under the tree root was dry and lined with fallen leaves. James, suddenly exhausted, got into his sleeping bag and curled up with Jack beside him. Fenella, purring loudly, jumped on to his lap and rubbed her head against him. "Tell him not to worry and to get some sleep," she told Jack. "I'll go home, find out what's happening and come back later." And she trotted daintily away.

The sun dipped below the horizon and the shadows deepened.

As night descended, the shapes of the trees on the heath began
to look menacing. James shivered. He felt wretched and
defeated. To keep up their spirits he opened a can of baked
beans and took out some slices of ham, a slab of cheese and a

chicken leg which he shared with Jack.

He had also filched some of his mother's chocolate from the fridge and they ate it greedily. When they realised they had very little food left for the morning, James said: "What do we do now, boy? What's going to happen?"

"Well," said Jack, "the police will probably use dogs to search for us which is both a good and a bad thing. Police dogs are nice intelligent animals but they take their work incredibly seriously. I don't know if I could count on them to put the police off the scent if they did find us. To make sure they do, I'm going to need some of your clothes. Put your socks in the plastic bag you used for the food. I'll go to the entrance of the heath now it's dark, tip out your socks and lay a completely false trail a long way from here. If I see any of my friends on the way being taken for a late walk I'll let them know what's happened. I'll get them to sound warning barks if they think we're in danger of being discovered."

"I feel so tired," said James, "I might just curl up in my sleeping bag when you're gone. Please don't take the slightest risk. It is you who are in the most danger and it's me who should be laying the false trail."

"You're too conspicuous," said Jack, "and you don't have my dog contacts. Go to sleep and when I come back I'll curl up beside you and speak to my special friend."

"Canis, King of the Dogs?" said James. "Will he help?"

"I hope so," said Jack. He snaked his way under the ivy and brambles that concealed them with the plastic bag in his mouth.

Jack was not convinced Canis would help. He hadn't been much help last time. Dog Lore emphatically said dogs must not bite humans.

On the other hand, it said a dog must be prepared to lay down his life for his master. "I don't want to die," thought Jack. "I'm frightened." He spent an hour laying his false trail, buried both socks in different parts of the heath and then returned to snuggle up against James dreading what the morning would bring.

■ **CHAPTER ELEVEN** ■

THE SEARCH BEGINS

The Pack Leader came back from her jaunt in London at about 5pm. The house was empty but she presumed James had gone out with his friends and Tom was shopping in town. When she heard Tom's car pull up in the drive she went out to greet him. As soon as she saw his expression, her smile died. He pointed to his arm which she saw was bandaged. "I need to talk to you," he said. "There have to be some big changes in this house." He stomped inside. She followed him resentfully.

"That dog you think so highly of has bitten me," said Tom. "I've just had a tetanus jab and got the wound dressed – it was a deep bite."

"Jack?" said the Pack Leader incredulously. "Jack would never bite anyone."

"Are you calling me a liar?" said Tom.

The Pack Leader's eyes narrowed. She'd seen flashes of his temper before and felt her own rising. She found it unbelievable that Jack could bite anyone. Her first instinct was to defend the pet she trusted with her son.

"Why did Jack bite you?" she said fighting to sound reasonable.

"I tried to get him off the sofa," lied Tom. "It's your fault he thinks he's allowed to be there in the first place."

"I'm sorry Jack bit you," said the Pack Leader, after taking a deep breath, "but trying to blame me isn't very helpful. You can't expect to come here and lay down the law and expect everyone to jump to your bidding. And that goes for me. Change takes time."

Tom's spiteful look shocked her. For the first time she saw the pent-up violence in him.

"I can't live in a house with a vicious dog," said Tom. "I'm sorry, but I can't. I know how much you think of him – you're a real softie – but he's snapped at me a couple of times before. I didn't say anything. I thought he'd settle down once he got used to me. As you've said yourself, you don't know what you're getting when you take an abandoned dog from kennels. You suspected he'd been treated badly. I know it's not his fault but sometimes it turns them vicious. This will upset you but you've got to have him put down – not for me, but for James' sake. He may bite him next, then how would you feel?"

The Pack Leader slumped on the sofa. She loved Jack.

"Perhaps he can be trained ...?"

Tom shook his head. "The dog was abused long before he came to you. How could you have known?"

He took her hands. "It's hard but it has to be your decision," he said gently. "Put the dog down as soon as possible. We can get another one and James will get over it in time."

But knowing her son and how he felt about Jack she seriously doubted it. "Where are Jack and James?" she said.

"I don't know," said Tom. "I'll go back to my flat now and leave you to think things over. I don't want to influence you."

When James did not return for his supper his mum became concerned and rang Kevin.

"No he didn't come out with us," said Kevin. "We haven't seen him at all today. We called at your house but Tom said he was tidying his bedroom."

When James hadn't returned by 10pm Kev's dad went up to the heath with a torch. He not only searched the den but the area around it. He had to return home and tell the Pack Leader he hadn't found James. She had phoned all her son's friends but no one had seen him or his dog. At 11pm, scared out of her wits, the Pack Leader dialled 999.

The policeman who soon arrived was Dennis, Nick the vet's brother. He took down all the details she could give and then said he would speak to Tom. Like her, he found it incredible that the big, soft animal he'd seen on the riverbank would bite anyone. "I'll get a team to search the heath," he told her, "I'm certain he'll be hiding there. James is a lovely kid. If he thinks his dog may be put down he'll be in a bit of a state."

Tom was only interested in showing Dennis the wound on his arm. He stuck to his story that Jack had attacked him when he tried to remove him from the sofa. When Dennis told him the boy and the dog hadn't come home, his only comment was: "That's typical of that spoilt little brat. He hasn't spared a thought for his mother."

"Well perhaps YOU could ring her or go round to comfort her," said Dennis. "She's pretty upset."

"I'm just about to go there now, thanks for asking," said Tom, looking the policeman up and down with hardly disguised disdain.

As he left, Dennis realised he disliked Tom with a passion.

Indeed, he was so angry that he decided to run his name through the police computer to see if he had ever been in trouble with the law. What he read dismayed him. Tom had assaulted a woman he had once lived with. The court had made an order forbidding him from going anywhere near her or her daughter. "So he's violent," thought Dennis. "I wonder if that is why Jack bit him?" He stared at the computer for a long time.

Then he phoned his brother Nick the vet who was horrified to hear that James had run away with Jack. "This is a bit of a long shot," began Dennis, "but I know you're their vet and I just wondered if you'd ever suspected someone was being cruel to Jack?" There was a long pause.

"Well, as it happens," said Nick, and he told Dennis about Jack's strange injury and how he'd suspected someone had kicked him.

"I'm only guessing now," said Dennis, "but perhaps Tom hurt the dog or even went for the boy. I've reason to believe the man could be violent. Between you and me, he's got a record for it. Do you think that dog would bite someone who attacked James?"

"Undoubtedly," said Nick. "Jack adores James and would do anything to protect him. And the feeling is mutual."

"I suspected that," said Dennis. "Where do you think they'll be hiding?"

"Somewhere on the heath," said Nick. "The trouble is it's a big place and James will know lots of secret places on it."

Later, with a heavy heart, Dennis had to report to James'

mum that the search team had not found James or Jack. Their top dog, Rex, had picked up a couple of trails but they turned out to be false. They would start searching again next morning.

Fenella watched the Pack Leader sob after she put down the phone. She simply could not let this state of affairs go on any longer. She racked her brains thinking of a way to help. James has to let her know he's all right, she thought. And that nice vet, Nick, has to learn the truth.

She hopped along the back fence to the end of the garden and started to caterwaul. Soon a large group of cats had clustered around her listening intently. Afterwards they dispersed, each going purposefully in a different direction.

In the hollow on the heath James was in a deep but fretful sleep, his fists clutching the end of his sleeping bag. Jack was beside him but he was wide awake. He was wondering what terrible things they would have to face next day.

■ CHAPTER TWELVE ■

STITCHING UP REX

Despite the comfy sleeping bag and Jack's warmth, James missed his socks. His cold feet kept waking him up. Every time he opened his eyes he felt utter confusion. He saw the stark silhouettes of the trees against the night sky instead of his familiar bedroom. When he remembered where he was and why, hopelessness descended on his shoulders like a cloak of iron.

But the night was not without incident or visitors. At around 10pm James woke in a panic when he realised Jack was no longer beside him. Then he saw him a few metres away in earnest conversation with an unfamiliar dog. When he called out, Jack trotted back.

"I'd like you to meet a friend – Brillo, the heath dog," said Jack. Then he lowered his voice and whispered: "I know you're not the sort of Human Being that judges by appearances but try not to be shocked at his."

"What's wrong with him?" asked James.

"Nothing, deep down," said Jack. "He's one of the kindest and nicest dogs I've ever met. But because he lives wild on the heath his coat's a bit of a mess. Also, he's got very few teeth but that's the fault of cruel Human Beings, not his. This hollow is his favourite home but he generously told Fenella we could stay here. Brillo may have next to nothing but what he's got he shares. He's also produced some very useful information." Jack gave a little bark and Brillo approached shyly.

"Hi, Brillo," said James. "Thanks for letting us use your home – it's a wonderful dry, secret place and we're very grateful." Brillo wagged his tail and then, confident he wasn't going to be sent packing, came and pushed his head against James' hand. Looking down, James could see the dog's fur was matted. Some had come off in clumps leaving ugly bald patches. But he was such an affectionate little fellow James did not hesitate to give Brillo the first good stroke he'd had in years. Brillo squirmed with the unaccustomed pleasure of human touch.

Rex the police dog had told Brillo the search for James and Jack would resume at dawn. Rex was a decent enough dog, said Brillo, but a bit of a jobsworth. There was no way he would lead his handler astray just to help another dog. The other bad news was that Rex had a phenomenally sensitive nose. Brillo did not doubt Rex would find them. James, already cold without his socks, was reluctant to part with any more clothing to lay more false trails.

"It's not necessary," said Jack, "for Brillo has a truly brilliant plan. He feels a bit rotten about doing this to Rex but he thinks his police career will survive and Rex may eventually thank him for it."

It emerged that Rex was in love with another Alsatian called Freda. She lived in a house whose fenced garden backed on to the heath. For almost a year the two dogs had flirted with each other through the fence. Now their dearest wish was to have puppies together.

"They're both handsome, pedigree animals and their puppies would be beautiful," said Jack. But Freda's owners had other plans. They kept a very close eye on her and had found her a partner with an impeccable pedigree to sire her pups. Freda did not care for him at all as she had given her heart to Rex. She was being taken to see this prospective partner tomorrow and was in despair.

"So where's this leading us?" said James, puzzled.

"It's where Freda will be leading Rex," said Jack with a chuckle.

"I still don't get it."

Jack explained that because Brillo had been forced to bury a lot of the stuff he found on the heath so other dogs didn't steal it, he had become a champion digger. Earlier that evening he'd started digging a hole under the fence around Freda's garden. "He's spoken to Freda," said Jack, "and she's well up for it. At first light she'll bark and demand to be let out. She'll escape on to the heath though Brillo's new tunnel and ....."

"Oh, how clever," said James. "Rex will see Freda and he won't be able to concentrate on finding us."

"Even better," said Jack, "he won't need to see her, his amazing nose will let him know she's around. Freda will persuade him to chase after her so they can spend a little private time together. It may be the only chance in their lives and Freda believes Rex will be unable to resist her."

"Brillo," said James, "your plan's fantastic." Brillo wagged with delight. He thought he might even be persuaded to give up his life as a free dog if only he had an owner like James to admire him.

James, with his uncanny understanding of the dog mind, told him: "If, and when, I get out of here, Brillo, I'll find you a good home – that's a promise."

Eventually Brillo left them to continue digging his tunnel under Freda's fence. James slumbered some more. When he next awoke, the sound of purring filled his ears. He saw Fenella had returned and was now curled up on his chest.

Fenella told Jack that Kev's mum was at the house comforting the Pack Leader. "She's very upset," said Fenella. "Tom told her you bit him, and she has to have you put down. He's tried to convince her you're vicious and can't be trusted. Just as she was getting her head round that, she realised you and James had run away. Dennis the policeman, the brother of that nice vet Nick, has been round."

James felt grey with guilt. He realised how upset his mother must be not knowing if he was dead or alive. He had a desperate urge to run home immediately. But the fear of what could happen to Jack if he did stopped him. "Poor mum," he said.

"You must let her know you're safe," said Jack.

"But how?"

Fenella scratched around in the dry leaves. Finally she produced a pen which she dumped on James' lap. "She carried it all the way from the house in her mouth," said Jack with grudging admiration.

"But we don't have any paper," said James. He and Jack

started to rummage around for something to write on. James found the empty baked beans can and started carefully to peel off the label. "I'll use the back," he said.

It was very difficult to see and James had ungainly, large handwriting. He managed to write: "Dear mum, don't worry. Jack and I are safe and well but I can't come home while ...." and then he ran out of paper.

"It's perfect," said Jack reassuringly, "you've said the most important things. Fold it up and Fenella will take It home in her mouth and leave it by the front door. The Pack Leader will think you sneaked home and posted it."

After Fenella left, James slept again, this time more deeply. When he woke the sun had just peeped above the horizon. He could hear the sound of men shouting to each other and the whack of sticks flattening grass. The search had resumed.

James lay stock still in his sleeping bag, his arms around Jack. They hardly dared to breathe as the voices got nearer. Jack's nose quivered in disgust as the smell of cigarette smoke wafted over their hideaway. Soon they could clearly hear the men's conversation.

"Don't know how a kid could hide out here all this time," said one man.

"Well, it's a big heath and he knows it well. Plays over here, apparently," said another. "But Rex will find him – he's got an amazing nose. Here he comes now with his handler. It looks as if he's got a scent. Look how he's pulling on his lead."

A third voice yelled: "Rex is on to something. I'm going to let him off so he can go with it."

James and Jack exchanged dismayed glances. Rex was now heading in their direction but where was Freda? Had Brillo's tunnel collapsed before she could escape? Jack dropped his head to his paws, depressed. James bit his bottom lip. Then suddenly they heard an angry, bemused voice shout: "Rex, what the ...?"

"Dog's gone mad," said another.

"Boy, he must have got a really powerful scent to go racing off like that."

"But it's in the opposite direction to where he was pulling first ..."

"Yes, that's a puzzle but who knows how dogs' noses work."

"He won't come back, though. Look at him run."

The voices got fainter and Jack and James grinned. "Brilliant Brillo," said James. He imagined poor Rex, blind to his duty for once and willing to risk his career for Freda, the love of his life.

Thanks to Freda they were not found by Rex. Apart from an occasional visit from the odd cat and dog it was a long, hot, boring day. Fenella breezed by in the late afternoon. She told them Kevin and John had been made to show the police the den by their parents. Cunningly, the pair had returned later and hidden food in it for Jack and James to eat later. "Brillo will bring it to us when it gets dark," said Jack.

"He looks like he needs a good meal more than we do," said James.

"He'd never steal, though," said Jack. "He's a very moral dog, but I'm sure he'd love something to eat. It would be a good way to thank him."

Kev and John had managed to filch a few roast potatoes, chicken leg, couple of Yorkshire puddings, slice of apple pie, dog biscuits and a leg of lamb bone from their homes. They had very fortunately wrapped each individual treat in silver foil. Brillo duly delivered the food. His eyes filled up when James insisted the lamb bone was his – in return for all the trouble he'd taken. Brillo tried to share the bone with Jack who, although dribbling copiously and privately thinking it was wasted on a dog with few teeth, nobly declined. After the three of them had eaten and the sky had begun to lose its colour there was nothing else to do but suffer another long, lonely night in the hollow on the heath.

■ CHAPTER THIRTEEN ■

WOOING AND WINNING McCARTHY

After leaving the heath Fenella deposited James' note by the front door. Afterwards, quite worn out by all her good works, she had a catnap, went on a brief hunt and then fell asleep at dawn. When she awoke late on Sunday morning she noticed the note had gone and the Pack Leader seemed slightly more cheerful. At least she knew her son was safe. Phase one of Fenella's plan had succeeded. Now it was time to move on to phase two.

Fenella jumped through the catflap and trotted lightly along the back fence to the end of the garden. She summoned her friends with an ear-splitting caterwaul. But as more and more cats arrived and glumly reported they'd failed in the mission she had set them Fenella started to get despondent. "I can't understand it," she confided to her best friend Miss E. Perkins. "A big ginger tom called McCarthy can't be that hard to find. Ginger toms are usually the most appalling extroverts. They love fighting, father scores of children and are ridiculously territorial. Someone must know him."

Miss E. broke off from her fastidious grooming. "That vet Nick could have been lying about having a cat," she said.

"I hadn't thought of that," said Fenella frowning. "Anything's possible with men but I didn't have him down as a liar. I'm not usually wrong about Human Beings. I always give them the doubt of the benefit until they prove me wrong."

Just then a bedraggled cat, who was a strange mixture of ginger and tabby, joined the group. "My name's Walter," he said. "I hear you're looking for McCarthy."

"Yes," said Fenella brightly. "Do you know him?"

"I don't know him," said Walter, "but he's my father and I know where he lives."

"Splendid," said Fenella, "I'll pay him a visit at once."

"I wouldn't do that," said Walter.

"Why ever not?"

"He's a recluse. He doesn't like visitors and hardly ever goes out. There's about forty of us kits scattered around. Most of us have never seen him. He says he doesn't want anything more to do with cats. He's gone native."

Walter explained that McCarthy had once belonged to a family who didn't look after him. He had taken to the streets to fend for himself. Then he was challenged over his territory by a newcomer called Tiger. In the bloody fight that followed McCarthy took a beating. After losing his eye and half an ear he crept behind a bush to die of his injuries and his shame.

"But he had nothing to be ashamed of," said Walter loyally. "Tiger was well fed, in top condition and fought really dirty. My dad had decked him and was walking away when Tiger sprang at him while his back was turned. He didn't have a chance."

Walter said the only reason McCarthy survived was because Nick the vet found him, took him in, got him stitched up and cared for him.

"Recluse or not," said Fenella, more intrigued than she

cared to admit, "I intend to visit him because I've a job I want him to do. Lead the way, Walter."

McCarthy was spending his day on the windowsill overlooking the balcony of Nick's first floor flat. His territory was now reduced to that one balcony and he guarded it ferociously, day and night. He allowed no other cat to walk on it.

When Fenella leapt up there from a nearby tree McCarthy was in a deep snooze. Undeterred, Fenella strutted up and down the balcony railings. She worked herself up into her mega-machinegun purr and tried to look her most alluring. Despite his ragged ear and one working eye she found McCarthy a handsome fellow. She decided to play to his maleness. Eventually he opened his one good eye. His look was hostile. "This is my balcony – push off," he hissed and shut his eye, though not tightly. Fenella smirked and continued to pace and preen. She knew he was secretly watching from under his half-closed eyelid.

"I told you," he said between clenched teeth.

"I know what you told me," said Fenella, "Both MY ears are working, but I've never been good at doing what I'm told. Anyway, I don't have all day to pussyfoot around. I need a favour that only you can provide," and she gave him her most seductive smirk and narrowed her eyes.

"I can't provide anything for anyone any more," said McCarthy bitterly.

"Oh rubbish," said Fenella, flicking her tail in irritation, "a big, handsome fellow like you." Despite his professed hostility she saw McCarthy square his shoulders and knew he was not entirely immune to her feline charms. "I know what happened to you," persisted Fenella, "and I can't see why you don't put it behind you and get on with your life. No one liked that Tiger. He'd never have beaten you if he'd fought fairly. Perhaps you don't know but a few days after your fight he was run over by a milk float. The indignity of it! That is hardly a glamorous end for a cat who prided himself on lightning reactions. You would never have let that happen to you."

"So he's dead," said McCarthy, lightening up.

"Quite dead," said Fenella. "There's no reason why you couldn't be top cat of the area again if you'd just stop this ridiculous self-pity. You've got nine lives like the rest of us, why give up at one? Now stop your nonsense and hop down off that windowsill and talk to me. I have a plan and I need a tough, intelligent cat like you to make it succeed."

Flattered and curious, McCarthy jumped down. Fenella told him what she wanted. All the while she rubbed his head with hers. She gracefully circled his body on tiptoes, furling her tail round his own. By the time she had finished, McCarthy would have lost his other eye for her.

"Well, that's settled then," she said finally, giving him no time to disagree. "Get Nick to the front door at 9pm and then just make him follow me and my friends."

■ CHAPTER FOURTEEN ■

THE BARK OF RESPECT

Although he was exhausted, Jack was too tense to sleep. After dark the heath came alive with many unfamiliar and potentially threatening noises as the nocturnal creatures who lived there emerged from trees, holes and burrows to hunt. Bats dipped and darted catching insects on the wing, their silhouettes flitting against the backdrop of a full moon. The ground creaked and leaves rustled as mice, rats and moles foraged for food and cats came out to stalk them.

Eventually, despite his unease, Jack felt his lids grow heavy. Soon the familiar breeze began to ripple through his fur. A veteran traveller to Kennelworth Castle, he felt almost relaxed as he was pulled upwards through the sky to the magic land of the cotton wool grass. I'm going to be put down, probably tomorrow, he thought with despair as he hurtled through the night sky. Whatever happens to me now, nothing could be worse than that.

He did not expect a warm welcome. He had broken Dog Lore, broken faith with dogs and Human Beings by biting someone. But in his heart he knew that if he ever thought James was in danger again he would behave in exactly the same way. His one regret, if he were honest, was that he hadn't given Tom an even harder bite to teach him never to be evil again.

The warm wind dropped. When he opened his eyes Jack saw

the familiar stream beside him and the Forest of a Thousand Sniffs. But there was no Bruno to greet him. I am truly in the dog house, he thought. But I might as well get on with it. With heavy paws he walked towards the forest. He was so preoccupied with his woes he hardly noticed its wonderful smells. The journey seemed endless. When he finally reached the castle there was not a single dog in sight. Sadly he approached the vast kennel and peered inside. When he realised he was quite alone he slumped at the entrance and put his head on his paws.

Suddenly the peace was ruptured by a deafening fanfare of trumpets. Dog upon dog slowly walked out of the forest, each one carrying a huge bone in its mouth. Closer and closer they came. As Jack shrank back, they formed a semi-circle round him. Then came another fanfare and the dogs parted to form a corridor. At the end of it he saw Bruno, Canis and Daisy. They approached carrying bones in their mouths. Canis's was so huge it looked as if it must have been torn from a Tyrannosaurus Rex.

Jack, now sitting rigidly upright, dropped his head as the silent trio came slowly nearer. The only sound was the muffled thumps of their legs touching the ground. It was worse than he thought. Jack looked down and soon felt the warm breath of Canis high above him. Three bones were gently placed before him.

"Jack, look at me," boomed Canis. Slowly Jack raised his head. He was puzzled to see Canis looking down at him with kindly eyes. "You have no reason to be ashamed, Jack," said

Canis. "We have come to honour, not to punish, you. Your bravery and selfless devotion to your master fills us with admiration. Yours is an example every dog should follow. We are proud of you, truly proud. Each dog here has spent the day trying to find the biggest bone they could as a mark of their esteem." Jack shook himself in disbelief. Canis dipped his head and Jack lifted his. They touched noses and suddenly the dogs broke out into a spontaneous volley known as The Bark of Respect.

"But I've broken Dog Lore," began Jack, hardly daring to believe what was happening.

"Only for the most honourable motives," said Canis. "You showed immense canine courage. You acted to defend James from that bully. You have survived your second test – you confronted and triumphed over evil. You did well, wonderfully well."

"But they're going to put me down for biting him. I'm not brave at all, I'm frightened," said Jack.

Canis, King of the Dogs, paused. He seemed to look into the distance. "I don't believe they will, Jack, when the truth comes out," he said. "And anyway, Jack, it's not your destiny. You have passed two crucial tests. You have one last test to undergo."

"I'm fed up with these wretched tests," retorted Jack sulkily. "Other dogs don't have to lay their lives on the line like I have. Surely I've done enough? I don't want to die, I don't want to leave James."

Canis looked down at Daisy inquiringly and the little Westie nodded. "Yes, you must prepare him," she said. "He has to know why his life has been so difficult and why, in the end, he has nothing to fear. He has earned the right to know."

Canis sighed. "You're right as usual. Come into the kennel with me, son."

Inside, he told an astounded Jack that his special destiny was to be the next Canis. The dogs had voted for him unanimously. He'd demonstrated his great bravery by heroically triumphing over his ordeal by water and by defending his young master from evil. However there was a final test to take. When Jack heard what it was and how brave he would have to be before he could be crowned King of the Dogs he felt weak with fear. "I don't think I can," he whispered. "I'm not brave enough. Really, I'm not."

"Yes you are, Jack. You're the bravest dog I have ever met," said Canis. "Trust me and trust yourself."

When Jack at last sped back to the world of Human Beings, so much had become clear that his heart felt strangely lighter. He knew that whatever terrors lay ahead he had the strength to face them. For now, all he had to do was to watch, wait and protect James lying in his sleeping bag beside him on the heath.

■ CHAPTER FIFTEEN ■

CAT'S EYE TRAIL

McCarthy was asleep on his favourite cushion by the window when Nick arrived home that night. The vet took a can of drink from the fridge and then emptied the contents of a cat food tin into McCarthy's bowl. When his cat had polished it off and cleaned his paws and head, Nick said, as he always did: "Want to go out on the balcony, Mac?"

It was what McCarthy always did – but not tonight. Instead, Nick was surprised to see him saunter over to the front door. He sat staring at it. When Nick did not respond, McCarthy began to scratch the paintwork.

"Heh," said Nick, "what's got into you?" But McCarthy remained stubbornly at the door gazing at the handle. "But you never want to go out, Mac," said Nick. Eventually he gave in and opened the door. McCarthy strode out and waited for Nick at the top of the stairs. "OK," said Nick, "I'll get my torch and coat, come down and let you out. I could really do without this tonight. I'm really tired."

He followed McCarthy downstairs and opened the front door to the flats. But when he shone his torch along the path that led out to the road he was astounded to see it was flanked by hundreds of little lights. When he concentrated his beam he saw they were not really lights but the eyes of scores of cats lining the walkway. McCarthy swaggered up the path lined with cats' eyes. An amazed Nick followed. Whenever he

stopped, so did McCarthy. Eventually he realised his cat was determined he should follow him. The cats' eyes also lined footpaths all the way to the heath.

"This is unreal," said Nick, "it's got to be a dream," but he was intrigued and felt compelled to follow. Over the hill they led him, through a wood and then another. Afterwards he had to hack his way through brambles and ivy. Suddenly all the lights went out. He thought he was quite alone.

He shone his torch in every direction and saw the base of a fallen tree on the bank in front of him. Its roots were wrenched from the ground. Beneath it was a hollow and there, sitting bolt upright as if on guard, was a large black dog. "Jack," Nick cried in relief. "It's me. Nick. Easy boy," and he approached at a crouch swinging brambles out of his way. He saw Jack's tail give little thumps of recognition. Nick stroked the dog's head and looked down at the sleeping bag beside him. "So you're guarding your little master like a good boy, are you?" he said. Jack's tail thumped some more. Nick moved nearer and peeled back the sleeping bag. He saw the tousled blond hair and, to his immense relief, heard breathing. He shone his torch on James' face and noticed he had dried blood under his nose.

Nick looked away and clenched his jaw, suppressing his rage. "I think I know why you bit Tom, Jack," he said softly and he noticed the dog's worried eyes lighten with relief, almost as if he'd understood. Gently he shook the sleeping boy and whispered: "Wake up James, it's over now, lad."

James, disorientated by sleep, shot upright and begun to burble "Got to run, got to hide, protect my dog ...."

"You haven't got to do anything, James, you can leave it to me," said Nick calmly. "What I do want you to do is tell me why you ran away." He put his arm around James. "In your own time, lad, in your own time."

"No one will believe me," said James.

"Try me," said Nick.

"It looked like Tom was going to hit me but I can't prove it," said James. "That's why Jack bit him. My mum'll think I'm making it up because I don't like Tom."

"Well, I'm staring at some pretty conclusive evidence." said Nick, shining his torch beam on James' face.

"What do you mean?"

"Did you know you've got a bloody nose?"

James shook his head and gingerly touched it. "I thought it felt a bit sore," he said.

"When your mum sees you, she'll want to know how you got hurt," said Nick.

"Jack only bit Tom to protect me," said James with passion, "but Tom said he'd make sure Jack got put down."

"Tom had no right to frighten you," said Nick.

"He thinks he has," said James. "My mum might believe his lies and I might lose Jack. I couldn't bear it, it's so unfair."

"Come on," said Nick, squeezing James' shoulder. "Let's go home. Tell your mum what you've told me. Have faith in her."

Nick took his mobile phone from his pocket and dialled. "Mrs Bentley," he said to James' mum, "it's Nick the vet. I've got James and Jack with me. They're safe and well and I'm bringing them back." Then Nick rang his brother Dennis at the police station and asked for a car. "A hot drink and blankets, too, if you can," he added. "OK boys," he said to Jack and James snapping shut his mobile, "time to go home."

■ CHAPTER SIXTEEN ■

HOMECOMING

The police car with its blue flashing light pulled up outside James' house. The Pack Leader, who'd been waiting at the window, flew out of the front door towards her son. He was draped in a big, grey blanket. Jack, reluctant to leave the back seat, looked past her towards Tom. He was silhouetted by the hall light at the front door, a cigarette in his hand. Then he watched the man chuck the butt on the lawn and saunter towards James and his mum. She was stroking her son's hair and hugging him hard. By now curtains had peeled back from other houses and neighbours had come out to witness James' homecoming.

"I've been out of my mind with worry, James," sobbed the Pack Leader. "Thank God you're safe. It's all that matters." Jack gingerly left the car and stood beside Nick and Dennis. Nick could feel the dog's trembling as he pressed against his leg. The vet stroked his head. "Don't worry, boy," he whispered. "Hang on in there."

The Pack Leader then held her son away from her and looked in shock at his face. "You've got dried blood under your nose," she said. "What's happened to you?"

James swallowed hard and his courage almost failed him as he saw Tom draw close. The man stood behind his mother staring at James over her shoulder. James dropped his eyes. He knew what he said now and how he said it meant the difference between life and death for his dog.

"Mum," he began, "Tom wouldn't let me go to the heath. When he caught me trying to sneak out of the house with Jack he went for me and I fell over. Jack thought Tom was going to hit me – so did I – and that's why he bit him. I swear it's the truth. You've got to believe me."

"That's quite an imagination you've got," said Tom coldy. "No such thing happened and you know it. I did insist you tidy your room. You did try to sneak out but you tripped over your dog and hit your head on the door frame. You are just trying to make me look bad. You've been used to having your mum to yourself and you can't bear to share her with anyone."

The Pack Leader straightened up and looked very deeply into James' eyes. Then she looked beyond him to Jack. He was sitting very squarely as if he was on parade, pressed up against the vet. Nick could feel him shaking but knew he could say nothing. This woman had to make a decision about who to believe and she had to make it without anyone else's help.

It seemed as if everyone in the tragic little tableau held their breath. Even the line of cats who had stolen through the night to sit on the fence and watch the outcome of the drama in which they had played a part.

The Pack Leader thought back to how they had found Jack at the kennels, of his gentleness and lack of aggression. She thought of Jack's mysterious injury. How Nick had told her privately that he thought the dog had been kicked. She knew deep down that neither Jack nor her cat ever wanted to be anywhere near Tom. When James had hinted at this she'd thought he was just jealous. Suddenly she knew who was telling the truth.

The Pack Leader narrowed her eyes, pursed her lips and seemed to struggle with some great anger. She wheeled round to face Tom.

"How dare you frighten my son?" she thundered. "How dare you try to rob him of his beloved dog? I don't believe your story. Get your things out of my house and never, ever come near me and my son again."

Tom opened his mouth to speak but seeing the Pack Leader's implacable anger, closed it again. He turned on his heels without a word but lit another cigarette as he went into the house. He knew they all hated the smell.

They waited in silence until he came out. He threw his suitcase into the back of his car and backed out of the drive. Before he left, he rolled down the window. He looked at James and his mother coldly and said: "You'll be sorry for this."

They watched the car disappear.

"I'll leave you then," said Dennis breaking the silence. The Pack Leader looked at him, all anger gone now. "I've got a lot to thank you for," she said. "And you Nick."

"There's someone else who deserves thanks, too," Nick added, looking down at Jack still pressed up against his leg.

"Oh yes, there most certainly is," she said in a husky voice. She knelt down and said gently: "Come here my beautiful boy. How could I ever have doubted you? Perhaps a specially big bone and a large plate of sausages will help you to forgive me?" Jack came shyly forward and pushed at her hands with his nose as she rubbed his silky fur. Suddenly he felt that enduring the human cruelty test had been worth it. James was safe, Tom was gone and he was surrounded by love.

Nick got into Dennis's police car. As he put on his headlights Dennis smiled wrily and told Nick to take a look at the fence in front of the car. His beam had caught a line of cats, including his brother's, looking down at them with studied interest. "Would you credit it," said Nick. "I sometimes think I know very little about animals, despite all my training. Even my cat McCarthy is there and he never goes out. It's unbelievable."

He stuck his head through the car window and shouted to James and his mum. "I might pop round – just to see how you all are." The Pack Leader raised her head and smiled. "Yes, that would be nice," she said.

James was worn out. He longed for his comfortable, warm bed. Sadly, he would be robbed of something far more precious than sleep that night. The next few hours would be the most dangerous of his life.

■ CHAPTER SEVENTEEN ■

THE FINAL TEST

If he hadn't been so exhausted Jack may have smelt the fire sooner. But suddenly he was wide awake, his nose quivering. There was a danger in the house greater than he'd ever known. He knew his final test had come. But for the first time in his life Jack felt brave. He had at last grown into a courageous dog. Just as Canis promised he would. Now he wasn't scared. He was determined.

"Wake up," he barked at James, roughly pulling his bedclothes. Confused, the boy, tired out by his time living rough on the heath, grudgingly stirred and began to cough. Jack grabbed his pyjama top with his mouth and yanked it.

"Oh, stop it. Leave me alone. I'm tired," said James and coughed some more. The bitter smell finally jolted him awake. He remembered his old dream and the fog that used to choke him. Only he knew now that it hadn't been fog – it had been smoke. This time the dream was real. He blinked. The air stung. Panic hit him. The doorway was a blur and there was a strange orange glow beyond. Flickering, frightening.

"Hold on to my fur," said Jack, "and I'll lead you to safety," just as the dog had said in his dream. He and Jack stumbled to the door together. When they opened it James saw flames eating the bannisters and carpet. "Now run," barked Jack croakily. "Don't look back. I'll go and get your mother." But James remained rooted to the spot. Jack got behind him. He butted the back of his knees hard. He shoved with all his strength so James lost his balance and almost fell towards the stairs.

Then suddenly the small figure he loved so much found the courage to run towards the flames and disappear.

Jack was quite alone now but he didn't linger. There was no time. Eyes smarting, he staggered along the landing. At last he reached the closed door of James' mother's bedroom. But although he strained against it, the door wouldn't budge. He got up on his hind legs and tried to turn the handle with his mouth. But that allowed even more smoke to pour into his already tortured lungs. He tried to bark a warning but his throat was too dry.

Clumsily he ran at the door, banging it with his broad head as hard as he could. Perhaps she would hear him and wake up? Again and again he pounded at the door until all his strength had gone and his legs buckled beneath him. Defeated, he sunk exhausted to the floor. He could no longer breathe.

Jack shut his sore eyes, smarting from the smoke, and felt a dizziness wash over him. He began to float away from the acrid smell and thick, suffocating air. Away from the despair that consumed him. He'd done his best. But he was so sad. He would have to break the solemn promise he'd made to James that he'd always look after him. His head sunk to his paws.

Then, quite suddenly, Jack was bathed in a wonderful calm. His ordeal by fire was over. It was the final test and he had now fulfilled his destiny. Miraculously the pain left him and a cool wind caressed his nose. His world began to spin and he was whisked away beyond the world of Human Beings to another, kinder world where dogs were never hurt and where he would wear a crown.

He was the new Canis, King of the Dogs.

■ CHAPTER EIGHTEEN ■

JACK'S MAGIC BENCH

James stumbled from the house choking. He saw the firemen rescue his mother through her bedroom window but kept anxiously watching the door for Jack. Where was he? Why didn't Jack come out? As the terrible truth began to dawn, James tried to run back for his dog. A fireman's strong arms stopped him and held him fast.

Wrapped in a red blanket he still watched the door. "Please come out, Jack. Please come out," he begged.

He heard a fireman say: "Looks like a cigarette did it to me."

But mum and I don't smoke, thought James. Then he remembered who did. Tom.

He tried to twist free from the fireman but he only tightened his grip. "You don't understand," said James. "My dog's in there. I've got to get him out."

"I'm sorry, son," said the fireman kindly. "I really am. But no one could survive that heat. We can't go in and I can't let you."

James no longer struggled when he was helped into an ambulance. The house was a charred wreck. He realised Jack would never come out now. Jack had saved him but it was too late to save Jack.

In the weeks that followed, James was inconsolable. Everyone told him he was lucky to be alive but James didn't feel lucky. Jack had died because of him. He couldn't get that out of his head.

He tried to get on with his life but everyone noticed how quiet he'd become. He seldom wanted to go out with his friends. Every time James saw a dog, any old dog, he would feel tears flood his eyes. He knew everyone was worried about him but he couldn't help it. He missed Jack so much.

He took care to avoid the heath for three months after the fire because he didn't want to see any dogs. But on one particular day he found himself walking towards it in spite of himself. He crested Kite Hill, and then turned right. He had no idea where he was going or why. His feet seemed to have a mind of their own. James realised he was now very near the place where he had hidden with Jack beneath the root of the fallen tree. It seemed such a long time ago.

As he peered through the brambles by the side of the path he spotted a pair of brown eyes. James leaned forward, saw the ragged grey and white fur surrounding them and knew he had found an old friend.

"Brillo," he called, delighted. "Is it really you, boy?" James realised with shame that he had forgotten all about the poor, half-starved heath dog that he had promised to find a home.

Brillo scrambled up to the path on his skinny legs and James squatted down so he could stroke him. It was painful but also quite wonderful to touch a dog again. When Brillo pressed his wet nose into James' hand the boy made a decision. "Would you like to come and live with me?" he asked. Brillo couldn't speak like Jack but he certainly seemed to understand. His thin tail started to wag furiously.

"Come on, then," said James straightening up. And he set off for home. But Brillo didn't move. After a few steps, when James realised the dog was not with him, he turned round. Brillo was sitting just where he had left him. Then, after looking straight into James' eyes, he trotted off in the opposite direction towards the lakes. Every so often he would turn round and wag to make sure James followed.

Puzzled, James did. The pair of them went across the bridge and Brillo headed towards a new bench overlooking the water. It was bathed in an uncanny golden glow. The dog went right up to it and jumped onto the seat.

As he got nearer James could see there was an inscription cut into the back of the bench. It read: "Thanks from all the happy dogs of the heath, especially Jack the labrador."

He stared at the words for a long time hardly believing what he saw. When he bent to read them again he became so dizzy he had to sit down on the bench beside Brillo. Suddenly he felt as if he had been lifted into a dream. Memories of Jack flooded his brain with a searing intensity, picture upon vivid picture of their life together. And as he sat trancelike, his eyes brimming with tears, he suddenly heard the voice of his dear old friend as if he was next to him.

"It's a magic bench, James," said Jack. "I've erected it in your honour. I can do that sort of thing now because they've made me Canis, King of the Dogs.

"We dogs feel you deserve special recognition. If all Human Beings were like you, the world would be a much better place for all of us. Any dog lover who sits on this bench will immediately be filled with memories of dogs they once knew who are still in their hearts. Any time you need to speak to me, just sit on it, shut your eyes and I'll be there. I promised I'd always look after you. I've fulfilled my destiny. This is how I can fulfil my promise to you."

To order more copies of Jack: King of the Dogs
call the publisher on +44 (0)845 123 3971

Did you remember to feed the cat?
Meet Boing-Boing the Bionic Cat, he doesn't need
feeding he just needs charging ...

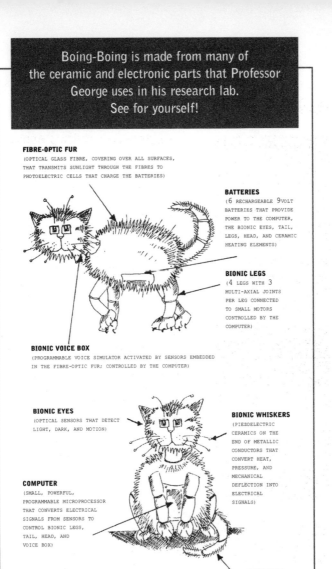

Boing-Boing is made from many of
the ceramic and electronic parts that Professor
George uses in his research lab.
See for yourself!

FIBRE-OPTIC FUR
(OPTICAL GLASS FIBRE, COVERING OVER ALL SURFACES,
THAT TRANSMITS SUNLIGHT THROUGH THE FIBRES TO
PHOTOELECTRIC CELLS THAT CHARGE THE BATTERIES)

BATTERIES
(6 RECHARGEABLE 9VOLT
BATTERIES THAT PROVIDE
POWER TO THE COMPUTER,
THE BIONIC EYES, TAIL,
LEGS, HEAD, AND CERAMIC
HEATING ELEMENTS)

BIONIC LEGS
(4 LEGS WITH 3
MULTI-AXIAL JOINTS
PER LEG CONNECTED
TO SMALL MOTORS
CONTROLLED BY THE
COMPUTER)

BIONIC VOICE BOX
(PROGRAMMABLE VOICE SIMULATOR ACTIVATED BY SENSORS EMBEDDED
IN THE FIBRE-OPTIC FUR; CONTROLLED BY THE COMPUTER)

BIONIC EYES
(OPTICAL SENSORS THAT DETECT
LIGHT, DARK, AND MOTION)

BIONIC WHISKERS
(PIEZOELECTRIC
CERAMICS ON THE
END OF METALLIC
CONDUCTORS THAT
CONVERT HEAT,
PRESSURE, AND
MECHANICAL
DEFLECTION INTO
ELECTRICAL
SIGNALS)

COMPUTER
(SMALL, POWERFUL,
PROGRAMMABLE MICROPROCESSOR
THAT CONVERTS ELECTRICAL
SIGNALS FROM SENSORS TO
CONTROL BIONIC LEGS,
TAIL, HEAD, AND
VOICE BOX)

BIONIC TAIL
(FOUR MULTI-AXIAL JOINTS THAT ENABLE TAIL TO MOVE
IN ALL DIRECTIONS UNDER COMPUTER CONTROL)

**Introduce someone you know to the fascination of robot-engineering -
and to a new friend, Boing-Boing the Bionic Cat.**

For further information on these titles please call the publisher or visit:
www.canofwormspress.co.uk

The Page Becomes the Stage

The Cartoon Shakespeare Series

cartoon*Shakespeare*

The complete, unexpurgated, text of Shakespeare's plays illustrated in full colour by world renowned artists/illustrators

"This series constitutes an excellent unpatronising introduction to Shakespeare."
The Financial Times

"Fabulous .... It could totally revolutionise children's attitudes to Shakespeare's plays."
The Yorkshire Post

"My VIth form are now addicts and I am regularly stopped in the corridors by a burly youth in the IVth form who wants to have another look at 'that Shakespeare book'..."
Teacher, St Aidans CofE High School

"Shakespeare's own poetic imagery is highlighted with masks, shadows, mirrors and creatures that stalk and lurk behind the brilliant, gaudy cartoon figures."
American Theatre

"Even if you don't understand some of the language you can follow what's happening from the expressions on the character's faces so you know when they feel happy, sad, angry, etc."
Student, Sanders Draper School

To order telephone: +44 (0) 845 123 3971
Email: sales@canofwormspress.co.uk or visit your
local bookstore on online bookseller.

The Page Becomes the Stage

Twelfth Night by William Shakespeare
The complete, unexpurgated, text of Shakespeare's
play illustrated in full colour by world renowned
artist/illustrator - John Howard.

ISBN: 1-904104-09-6 RRP £9.99
136 pages 208 mm x 140 mm

"Wonderful cartoon version – Viola in black
leather, Olivia as a vamp, Sir Toby Belch clutching
a copy of Sporting Life – from the talented studio
of John Howard."
The Catholic Herald

Othello by William Shakespeare
The complete, unexpurgated, text of Shakespeare's
play illustrated in full colour by world renowned
artist/illustrator - Oscar Zarate.

ISBN:1-904104-08-8 RRP £9.99
136 pages 208 mm x 140 mm

"It's a marvellous twitchy performance from
Zarate's cartoon Othello ... the more anxious the
hero, the closer the artist follows his darting
eyes...."
The Guardian

For further information on these titles please call the publisher or visit:
www.canofwormspress.co.uk